A CRISIS ON EVERY PLANET

The human race had spread through the galaxy, colonizing hundreds of alien worlds. The Interstellar Medical Service sent its scouts out to take whatever action was necessary to maintain peace, health and security on those worlds.

Calhoun was a medic, and on every planet he found nothing but trouble. On Talien III, he had to fight an alien chemical that was turning men into psychopathic killers. On Maya, he discovered vicious bio-weapons being used by a criminal cartel to control people as though they were cattle. On Phaedra II, he encountered a world of children, riddled with disease, yet pursuing a deadly interplanetary war.

Wherever he went, Calhoun had the same grim choice—avert danger and bring peace, or be destroyed himself by the very forces of chaos he was seeking to overcome!

DOCTOR TO THE STARS

Three novelettes of the Interstellar Medical Service

Murray Leinster

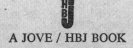

A JOVE / HBJ BOOK

First Jove/HBJ edition published December 1977

Printed in Canada

Jove/HBJ books are published by Jove Publications, Inc. (Har-
court Brace Jovanovich), 757 Third Avenue, New York, N.Y.
10017.

Contents

THE GRANDFATHERS' WAR

7

MED SHIP MAN

75

TALLIEN THREE

120

THE GRANDFATHERS' WAR

I.

" . . . No man can be fully efficient if he expects praise or appreciation for what he does. The uncertainty of this reward, as experienced, leads to modification of one's actions to increase its probability . . . If a man permits himself the purpose of securing admiration, he tends to make that purpose primary and the doing of his proper work secondary. This costs human lives . . ."
Manual, Interstellar Medical Service. Pp. 17-18.

The little Med Ship seemed absolutely motionless when the hour-off warning whirred. Then it continued to seem motionless. The background-noise tapes went on, making the small, unrelated sounds that exist unnoticed in all the places where human beings dwell, but which have to be provided in a ship in overdrive so a man doesn't go ship-happy from the dead stillness. The hour-off warning was notice of a change in the shape of things.

Calhoun put aside his book—the manual of the Med Service—and yawned. He got up from his bunk to tidy ship. Murgatroyd, the *tormal*, opened his eyes and regarded him drowsily, without uncoiling his furry tail from about his nose.

"I wish," said Calhoun critically, "that I could act with your realistic appraisal of facts, Murgatroyd! This is a case of no importance whatever, and you treat it as such, while I fume whenever I think of its futility. We are a token mission, Murgatroyd—a politeness of the Med

Service, which has to respond to hysterical summonses as well as sensible ones. Our time is thrown away!"

Murgatroyd blinked somnolently. Calhoun grinned wryly at him. The Med ship was a fifty-ton space-vessel —very small indeed, in these days—with a crew consisting exclusively of Calhoun and Murgatroyd the *tormal*. It was one of those little ships the Med Service tries to have call at every colonized planet at least once in four or five years. The idea is to make sure that all new developments in public health and individual medicine will spread as widely and as fast as can be managed. There were larger Med craft to handle dangerous situations and emergencies of novel form. But all Med Ships were expected to handle everything possible, if only because space travel consumed such quantities of time.

This particular journey, for example: An emergency message had come to Sector Headquarters from the planetary government of Phaedra II. Carried on a commercial vessel in overdrive at many times the speed of light, it had taken three months to reach Headquarters. And the emergency in which it asked aid was absurd. There was, said the message, a state of war between Phaedra II and Canis III. Military action against Canis III would begin very shortly. Med Service aid for injured and ill would be needed. It was therefore requested at once.

The bare idea of war, naturally, was ridiculous. There could not be war between planets. Worlds communicated with each other by spaceships, to be sure, but the Lawlor interplanetary drive would not work save in unstressed space, and of course overdrive was equally inoperable in a planet's gravitational field. So a ship setting out for the stars had to be lifted not less than five planetary diameters from the ground before it could turn on any drive of its own. Similarly, it had to be lowered an equal distance to a landing after its drive became unusable. Space travel was practical only because there were landing grids—those huge structures of steel which

8

used the power of a planet's ionosphere to generate the force-fields for the docking and launching of ships of space. Hence landing grids were necessary for landings. And no world would land a hostile ship upon its surface. But a landing grid could launch bombs or missiles as well as ships, and hence could defend its planet, absolutely. So there could be no attacks and there could be defense, so wars could not be fought.

"The whole thing's nonsense," said Calhoun. "We'll get there, and we've been three months on the way and the situation is six months old and either it's all been compromised or it's long forgotten and nobody will like being reminded of it. And we've wasted our time and talents on a thankless job that doesn't exist, and couldn't! The universe has fallen on evil days, Murgatroyd! And we are the victims!"

Murgatroyd leisurely uncurled his tail from about his nose. When Calhoun talked at such length, it meant sociability. Murgatroyd got up, and stretched, and said, "*Chee!*" He waited. If Calhoun really meant to go in for conversation, Murgatroyd would join in. He adored pretending that he was a human. He and his kind imitated human actions as parrots imitated human speech. Murgatroyd frisked a little, to show his readiness for talk.

"*Chee-chee-chee!*" he said conversationally.

"I notice that we agree," said Calhoun. "Let's clean up."

He began those small items of housekeeping which one neglects when nothing can happen for a long time ahead. Books back in place. Files restored to order. The special-data reels Calhoun had been required to study. Calhoun made all neat and orderly against landing and possible visitors.

Presently the breakout clock indicated twenty-five minutes more in overdrive. Calhoun yawned again. As an interstellar service organization, the Med Service sometimes had to do rather foolish things. Governments run by politicians required them. Yet Med Service representatives always had to be well-informed on problems which appeared. During this journey Calhoun had been ordered to read up on the ancient insanity once called the art of war. He didn't like what he'd learned about the doings of his ancestors. He reflected that it was lucky that such things couldn't happen anymore. He yawned again.

He was strapped in the control-chair a good ten minutes before the ship was due to return to a normal state of things. He allowed himself the luxury of still another yawn. He waited.

The warning tape whirred a second time. A voice said, "*When the gong sounds, breakout will be five seconds off.*" There was a heavy, rhythmic tick-tocking. It went on and on. Then the gong and a voice said: "*Five—four—three—t—*"

It did not complete the count. There was a tearing, rending noise and the spitting of an arc. There was the smell of ozone. The Med Ship bucked like a plunging horse. It came out of overdrive two seconds ahead of time. The automatic, emergency-rockets roared and it plunged this way and changed course violently and plunged that, and seemed to fight desperately against something that frustrated every maneuver it tried. Calhoun's hair stood on end until he realized that the external-field indicator showed a terrific artificial force-field gripping the ship. He cut off the rockets as their jerkings tried to tear him out of his chair.

There was stillness. Calhoun rasped into the space-phone:

"What's going on? This is Med Ship *Esclipus Twenty!* This is a neutral vessel!" The term "neutral vessel" was new in Calhoun's vocabulary. He'd learned it while studying the manners and customs of war in overdrive. "Cut off those force-fields!"

Murgatroyd shrilled indignantly. Some erratic movement of the ship had flung him into Calhoun's bunk,

10

where he'd held fast to a blanket with all four paws. Then another wild jerking threw him and the blanket together into a corner, where he fought to get clear, chattering bitterly the while.

"We're noncombatants!" snapped Calhoun—another new term.

A voice growled out of the spacephone speaker.

"Set up for light-beam communication," it said heavily. *"In the meantime keep silence."*

Calhoun snorted. But a Med Ship was not an armed vessel. There were no armed vessels nowadays. Not in the normal course of events. But vessels of some sort had been on the watch for a ship coming to this particular place.

He thought of the word "blockade"—another part of his education in the outmoded art of war. Canis III was blockaded.

He searched for the ship that had him fast. Nothing. He stepped up the magnification of his visionscreens. Again nothing. The sun Canis flamed ahead and below, and there were suspiciously bright stars which by their coloring were probably planets. But the Med Ship was still well beyond the habitable part of a sol-class sun's solar system.

Calhoun pulled a photocell out of its socket and waited. A new and very bright light winked into being. It wavered. He stuck the photocell to the screen, covering the brightness. He plugged in its cord to an audio amplifier. A dull humming sounded. Not quite as clearly as a spacephone voice, but clear enough, a voice said:

"If you are Med Ship Esclipus Twenty, answer by light beam, quoting your orders."

Calhoun was already stabbing another button, and somewhere a signal-lamp was extruding itself from its recess in the hull. He said irritably:

"I'll show my orders, but I do not put on performances of dramatic readings! This is the devil of a business! I came here on request, to be a ministering angel or a lady

11

with a lamp, or something equally improbable. I did not come to be snatched out of overdrive, even if you have a war on. This is a Med Ship!"

The slightly blurred voice said as heavily as before:

"This is a war, yes. We expected you. We wish you to take our final warning to Canis III. Follow us to our base and you will be briefed."

Calhoun said tartly:

"Suppose you tow me! When you dragged me out of overdrive you played the devil with my power!"

Murgatroyd said, *"Chee?"* and tried to stand on his hind legs to look at the screen. Calhoun brushed him away. When acknowledgment came from the unseen other ship, and the curious cushiony drag of the towing began to be felt, he cut off the microphone to the light-beam. Then he said severely to Murgatroyd:

"What I said was not quite true, Murgatroyd. But there is a war on. To be a neutral I have to appear impressively helpless. That is what neutrality means."

But he was far from easy in his mind. Wars between worlds were flatly impossible. The facts of space travel made them unthinkable.

Yet there seemed to be a war. Something was happening, anyhow, which was contrary to all the facts of life in modern times. And Calhoun was involved in it. It demanded that he immediately change all his opinions and all his ideas of what he might have to do. The Med Service could not take sides in a war, of course. It had no right to help one side or the other. Its unalterable function was to prevent the needless death of human beings. So it could not help one combatant to victory. On the other hand it could not merely stand by, tending the wounded, and by alleviating individual catastrophes allow their number to mount.

"This," said Calhoun, "is the devil!"

"Chee!" said Murgatroyd.

The Med Ship was being towed. Calhoun had asked

12

for it and it was being done. There should have been no way to tow him short of a physical linkage between ships. There were force-fields which could perform that function—landing grids used them constantly—but ships did not mount them—not ordinary ships, anyhow. That fact bothered Calhoun.

"Somebody's gone to a lot of trouble," he said, scowling, "as if wars were going back into fashion and somebody was getting set to fight them. Who's got us, anyhow?"

The request for Med Service aid had come from Phaedra II. But the military action—if any—had been stated to be due on Canis III. The flaming nearby sun and its family of planets was the Canis solar system. The odds were, therefore, that he'd been snatched out of overdrive by the Phaedrian fleet. He'd been expected. They'd ordered him not to use the spacephone. The local forces wouldn't care if the planet overheard. The invaders might. Unless there were two space fleets in emptiness, jockeying for position for a battle in the void. But that was preposterous. There could be no battles in unstressed space where any ship could flick into overdrive flight in the fraction of a second!

"Murgatroyd," said Calhoun querulously, "this is all wrong! I can't make head or tail or anything! And I've got a feeling that there is something considerably more wrong than I can figure out! At a guess, it's probably a Phaedrian vessel that's hooked on to us. They didn't seem surprised when I said who I was. But—"

He checked his instrument board. He examined the screens. There were planets of the yellow sun, which now was nearly dead ahead. Calhoun saw an almost infinitely thin crescent, and knew that it was the sunward world toward which he was being towed. Actually, he didn't need a tow. He'd asked for it for no particular reason except to put whoever had stopped him in the wrong. To injure a Med Ship would be improper even in war—especially in war.

13

His eyes went back to the external-field dial. There was a force-field gripping the ship. It was of the type used by landing grids—a type impractical for use on shipboard. A grid to generate such a force-field had to have one foot of diameter for roughly every ten miles of range. A ship to have the range of his captor would have to be as big as a planetary landing grid. And no planetary landing grid could handle it.

Then Calhoun's eyes popped open and his jaw dropped.

"Murgatroyd!" he said, appalled. "Confound them, it's true! They've found a way to fight!"

Wars had not been fought for many hundreds of years, and there was no need for them now. Calhoun had only lately been studying the records of warfare in all its aspects and consequences, and as a medical man he felt outraged. Organized slaughter did not seem a sane process for arriving at political conclusions. The whole galactic culture was based upon the happy conviction that wars could never happen again. If it was possible, they probably would. Calhoun knew humanity well enough to be sure of that.

"*Chee?*" said Murgatroyd inquiringly.

"You're lucky to be a *tormal!*" Calhoun told him. "You never have to feel ashamed of your kind."

The background information he had about warfare in general made him feel skeptical in advance about the information he would presently be given. It would be what used to be called propaganda, given him under the name of briefing. It would agree with him that wars in general were horrible, but it would most plausibly point out—with deep regret—that this particular war, fought by this particular side, was both admirable and justified.

"Which," said Calhoun darkly, "I wouldn't believe even if it were true!"

14

II.

"Information secured from others is invariably inaccurate in some fashion. A complete and reasoned statement of a series of events is almost necessarily trimmed and distorted and edited, or it would not appear reasonable and complete. Truly factual accounts of any series of happenings will, if honest, contain inconsistent or irrational elements. Reality is far too complex to be reduced to simple statements without much suppression of fact ..."

Manual, Interstellar Medical Service. P. 25.

He was able to verify his guess about the means by which interstellar war became practical, when the Med Ship was landed. Normally, a landing grid was a gigantic, squat structure of steel girders, half a mile high and a full mile in diameter. It rested upon bedrock, was cemented into unbreakable union with the substance of its planet, and tapped the ionosphere for power. When the Med Ship reached the abysmal darkness of the nearest planet's shadow, there were long, long pauses in which it hung apparently motionless in space. There were occasional vast swingings, as if something reached out and made sure where it was. And Calhoun made use of his nearest-object indicator and observed that something very huge fumbled about and presently became stationary in emptiness, and then moved swiftly and assuredly down into the blackness which was the planet's night-side. When it and the planetary surface were one, the Med Ship began its swift descent in the grip of landing grid-type force-fields.

It landed in the center of a grid—but not a typical grid. This was more monstrous in size than any spaceport boasted. It was not squat, either, but as tall as it was wide. As the ship descended, he saw lights in a control-system cell, midway to the ground. It was amazing but obvious. The Med Ship's captors had built a landing grid which was itself a spaceship. It was a grid which could cross the void between stars. It could wage offensive war.

"It's infernally simple," Calhoun told Murgatroyd. distastefully. "The regular landing grid hooks onto something in space and pulls it to the ground. This thing hooks onto something on the ground and pushes itself out into space. It'll travel by Lawlor or overdrive, and when it gets somewhere it can lock onto any part of another world and pull itself down to that and stay anchored to it. Then it can land the fleet that traveled with it. It's partly a floating dry dock and partly a landing craft, and actually it's both. It's a ready-made spaceport anywhere it chooses to land. Which means that it's the deadliest weapon in the past thousand years!"

Murgatroyd climbed on his lap and blinked wisely at the screens. They showed the surroundings of the now-grounded Med Ship, standing on its tail. There were innumerable stars overhead. All about, there was the whiteness of snow. But there were lights. Ships at rest lay upon the icy ground.

"I suspect," growled Calhoun, "that I could make a dash on emergency rockets and get behind the horizon before they could catch me. But this is just a regular military base!"

He considered his recent studies of historic wars, of battles and massacres and looting and rapine. Even modern, civilized men would revert very swiftly to savagery once they had fought a battle. Enormities unthinkable at other times would occur promptly if men went back to barbarity. Such things might already be present in the minds of the crews of these spaceships.

"You and I, Murgatroyd," said Calhoun, "may be the only wholly rational men on this planet. And you aren't a man."

"*Chee!*" shrilled Murgatroyd. He seemed glad of it.

"But we have to survey the situation before we attempt

16

anything noble and useless," Calhoun observed. "But still—what's that?"

He stared at a screen which showed lights on the ground moving toward the Med Ship. They were carried by men on foot, walking on the snow. As they grew nearer it appeared that there were also weapons in the group. They were curious, ugly instruments—like sporting rifles save that their bores were impossibly large. They would be— Calhoun searched his new store of information. They would be launchers of miniature rockets, capable of firing small missiles with shaped charges which could wreck the Med Ship easily.

Thirty yards off, they separated to surround the ship. A single man advanced.

"I'm going to let him in, Murgatroyd," observed Calhoun. "In war time, a man is expected to be polite to anybody with a weapon capable of blowing him up. It's one of the laws of war."

He opened both the inner and outer lock doors. The glow from inside the ship shone out on white, untrodden snow. Calhoun stood in the opening, observing that as his breath went out of the outer opening it turned to white mist.

"My name is Calhoun," he said curtly to the single dark figure still approaching. "Interstellar Medical Service. A neutral, a noncombatant, and at the moment very much annoyed by what has happened!"

A gray-bearded man with grim eyes advanced into the light from the opened port. He nodded.

"My name is Walker," he said, as curtly. "I suppose I'm the leader of this military expedition. At least, my son is the leader of the . . . ah . . . the enemy, which makes me the logical man to direct the attack upon them."

Calhoun did not quite believe his ears, but he pricked them up. A father and son on opposite sides would hardly have been trusted by either faction, as warfare used to be conducted. And certainly their relationship would hardly be a special qualification for leadership at any time.

He made a gesture of invitation, and the gray-bearded man climbed the ladder to the port. Somehow he did not lose the least trace of dignity in climbing. He stepped solidly into the air lock and on into the cabin of the ship.

"If I may, I'll close the lock-doors," said Calhoun, "if your men won't misinterpret the action. It's cold outside."

The sturdy, bearded man shrugged his cape-clad shoulders.

"They'll blast your ship if you try to take off," he said. "They're in the mood to blast something!"

With the same air of massive confidence, he moved to a seat. Murgatroyd regarded him suspiciously. He ignored the little animal.

"Well?" he said impatiently.

"I'm Med Service," said Calhoun. "I can prove it. I should be neutral in whatever is happening. But I was asked for by the planetary government of Phaedra. I think it likely that your ships come from Phaedra. Your grid ship, in particular, wouldn't be needed by the local citizens. How does the war go?"

The stocky man's eyes burned.

"Are you laughing at me?" he demanded.

"I've been three months in overdrive," Calhoun reminded him. "I haven't heard anything to laugh at in longer than that. No."

"The . . . our enemy," said Walker bitterly, "consider that they have won the war! But you may be able to make them realize that they have not, and they cannot. We have been foolishly patient, but we can't risk forbearance any longer. We mean to carry through to victory even if we arrive at cutting our own throats for a victory celebration! And that is not unlikely!"

Calhoun raised his eyebrows. But he nodded. His studies had told him that a war psychology was a highly emotional one.

"Our home planet Phaedra has to be evacuated," said Walker, very grimly indeed. "There are signs of instability in our sun. Five years since, we sent our older children to Canis III to build a world for all of us to move to. Our sun could burst at any time. It is certain to flare up some time—and soon! We sent our children because the place of danger was at home. We urged them to work feverishly. We sent the young women as well as the men at the beginning, so that if our planet did crisp and melt when our sun went off there would still be children of our children to live on. When we dared—when they could feel and shelter them—we sent younger boys and girls to safety, overburdening the new colony with mouths to feed, but at the least staying ourselves where the danger was! Later we sent even the small children, as the signs of an imminent cataclysm became more threatening."

Calhoun nodded again. There were not many novas in the galaxy in any one year, even among the millions of billions of stars it held. But there had been at least one colony which had had to be shifted because of evidence of solar instability. The job in that case was not complete when the flareup came. The evacuation of a world, though, would never be an easy task. The population had to be moved light-years of distance. Space-travel takes time, even at thirty times the speed of light. Where the time of disaster—the deadline for removal—could not be known exactly, the course adopted by Phaedra was logical. Young men and women were best sent off first. They could make new homes for themselves and for others to follow them. They could work harder and longer for the purpose than any other age-group—and they would best assure the permanent survival of somebody! The new colony would have to be a place of frantic, unresting labor, of feverish round-the-clock endeavor, because the time-scale for working was necessarily unknown but was extremely unlikely to be enough. When they could be burdened further, younger boys and girls would be shipped—old enough to help but not to pioneer. They could be sent to safety in a partly-built colony. Later smaller children could be sent, needing care from their older contemporaries. Only at long last would the adults leave their world for the new. They would stay where the danger was until all younger ones were secure.

"But now," said Walker thickly, "our children have made their world and now they refuse to receive their parents and grandparents! They have a world of young people only, under no authority but their own. They say that we lied to them about the coming flare of Phaedra's sun: that we enslaved them and made them use their youth to build a new world we now demand to take over! They are willing for Phaedra's sun to burst and kill the rest of us, so they can live as they please without a care for us!"

Calhoun said nothing. It is a part of medical training to recognize that information obtained from others is never wholly accurate. Conceding the facts, he would still be getting from Walker only one interpretation of them. There is an instinct in the young to become independent of adults, and an instinct in adults to be protective past all reason. There is, in one sense, always a war between the generations on all planets, not only Phaedra and Canis III. It is a conflict between instincts which themselves are necessary—and perhaps the conflict as such is necessary for some purpose of the race.

"They grew tired of the effort building the colony required," said Walker, his eyes burning as before. "So they decided to doubt its need! They sent some of their number back to Phaedra to verify our observations of the sun's behavior. Our observations! It happened that they came at a time when the disturbances in the sun were temporarily quiet. So our children decided that we were overtimid; that there was no danger to us; that we demanded too much! They refused to build more

20

shelters and to clear and plant more land. They even refused to land more ships from Phaedra, lest we burden
them with more mouths to feed! They declared for rest;
for ease! They declared themselves independent of us!
They disowned us! Sharper than a serpent's tooth . . ."

". . . Is an ungrateful child," said Calhoun. "So I've
heard. So you declared war."

"We did!" raged Walker. "We are men! Haven't we
wives to protect? We'll fight even our children for the
safety of their mothers! And we have grandchildren—on
Canis III! What's happened and is happening there . . .
what they're doing—" He seemed to strangle on his fury.
"Our children are lost to us. They've disowned us. They'd
destroy us and our wives, and they destroy themselves,
and they will destroy our grandchildren—We fight!"

Murgatroyd climbed into Calhoun's lap and cuddled
close against him. *Tormals* are peaceful little animals.
The fury and the bitterness in Walker's tone upset Murgatroyd. He took refuge from anger in closeness to Calhoun.

"So the war's between you and your children and
grandchildren," observed Calhoun. "As a Med Ship man
—what's happened to date? How has the fighting gone?
What's the state of things right now?"

"We've accomplished nothing," rasped Walker. "We've
been too softhearted! We don't want to kill them—not
even after what they've done! But they are willing to kill
us! Only a week ago we sent a cruiser in to broadcast
propaganda. We considered that there must be some
decency left even in our children! No ship can use
any drive close to a planet, of course. We sent the
cruiser in on a course to form a parabolic semiorbit,
riding momentum down close to atmosphere above Canopolis, where it would broadcast on standard communication frequencies and go on out to clear space again.
But they used the landing grid to strew its path with
rocks and boulders. It smashed into them. Its hull was
punctured in fifty places! Every man died!"

Calhoun did not change expression. This was an interview to learn the facts of a situation in which the Med Service had been asked to act. It was not an occasion in which to be horrified. He said:

"What did you expect of the Med Service when you asked for its help?"

"We thought," said Walker, very bitterly indeed, "that we would have prisoners. We prepared hospital ships to tend our children who might be hurt. We wanted every possible aid in that. No matter what our children have done—"

"Yet you have no prisoners?" asked Calhoun.

He didn't grasp this affair yet. It was too far out of the ordinary for quick judgment. Any war, in modern times, would have seemed strange enough. But a full-scale war between parents and children on a planetary scale was a little too much to grasp in all its implications in a hurry.

"We've one prisoner," said Walker scornfully. "We caught him because we hoped to do something with him. We failed. You'll take him back. We don't want him! Before you go, you will be told our plans for fighting; for the destruction, if we must, of our own children! But it is better for us to destroy them than to let them destroy our grandchildren as they are doing!"

This accusation about grandchildren did not seem conceivably true. Calhoun, however, did not question it. He said reflectively:

"You're going about this affair in a queer fashion, whether as a war or an exercise in parental discipline. Sending word of your plans to one's supposed enemy, for instance—"

Walker stood up. His cheek twitched.

"At any instant now, Phaedra's sun may go! It may have done so since we heard. And our wives—our children's mothers—are on Phaedra. If our children have murdered them by refusing them refuge, then we will have nothing left but the right—"

22

There was a pounding on the airlock door.

"I'm through," rasped Walker. He went to the lock and opened the doors. "This Med man," he said to those outside, "will come and see what we've made ready. Then he'll take our prisoner back to Canis. He'll report what he knows. It may do some good."

He stepped out of the airlock, flinging a command to Calhoun to follow.

Calhoun grunted to himself. He opened a cabinet and donned heavy winter garments. Murgatroyd said *"Chee!"* in alarm when it appeared that Calhoun was going to leave him. Calhoun snapped his fingers and Murgatroyd leaped up into his arms. Calhoun tucked him under his coat and followed Walker down into the snow.

This, undoubtedly, was the next planet out from the colonized Canis III. It would be Canis IV, and a very small excess of carbon dioxide in its atmosphere would keep it warmer—by the greenhouse effect—than its distance from the local sun would otherwise imply. The snow was winter snow only. This was not too cold a base for military operations against the planet next inward toward the sun.

Walker strode ahead toward the rows of spaceship hulls about the singularly spidery grip ship. It occured to Calhoun that astrogating such a ship would be very much like handling an oversized, open-ended wastebasket. A monstrous overdrive field would be needed, and keeping its metal above brittle-point on any really long space voyage would be difficult indeed. But it was here. It had undoubtedly lifted itself from Phaedra. It had landed itself here, and should be able to land on Canis and then let down after itself the war fleet now clustered about its base. But Calhoun tried to take comfort in the difficulty of traveling really long distances, up in the tens or twenties of light-years, with such a creation. Possibly, just possibly, warfare would still be limited to relatively nearby worlds—

"We thought," rumbled Walker, "that we might excavate shelters here, so we could bring the rest of Phaedra's population here to wait out the war—so they'd be safe if Phaedra's sun blew. But we couldn't feed them all. So we have to blast a reception for ourselves on the world our children have made!"

They came to a ship which was larger than any except the grid ship. Nearby half its hull had been opened and a gigantic tent set up against it. It was a huge machine shop. A spaceship inside was evidently the cruiser of which Walker had spoken. Calhoun could see where ragged old holes had been made in its hull. Men of middle age or older worked upon it with a somehow dogged air. But Walker pointed to another object, almost half the size of the Med Ship. Men worked on that, too. It was a missile, not man-carrying, with relatively enormous fuel-capacity for drive-rockets.

"Look that over," commanded Walker. "That's a rocket-missile, a robot fighting machine that we'll start from space with plenty of rocket-fuel for maneuvering. It will fight and dodge its way down into the middle of the grid at Canopolis—which our children refuse to use to land their parents. In three days from now we use this to blast that grid and as much of Canopolis as may go with it from the blast of a megaton bomb. Then our grid ship will land and our fleet will follow it down, and we'll be aground on Canis with blast-rifles and flame and more bombs, to fight for our rightful foothold on our children's world!

When our fighting men are landed, our ships will begin to bring in our wives from Phaedra—if they are still alive—while we fight to make them safe. We'll fight our children as if they were wild beasts—the way they've treated us! We begin this fight in just three days, when that missile is ready and tested. If they kill us—so much the better! But we'll make them do their murder with their hands, with their guns, with the weapons they'd doubtless made. But they shall not murder us by disowning us! And if we have to kill them to save our

24

grandchildren—we begin to do so in just three days! Take them that message!"

Calhoun said:

"I'm afraid they won't believe me."

"They'll learn they must!" growled Walker. Then he said abruptly: "What repairs does your ship need? We'll bring it here and repair it, and then you'll take our prisoner and carry him and your message back to his own kind—our children!"

The irony and the fury and the frustration in his tone as he said, "children," made Murgatroyd wriggle, underneath Calhoun's coat.

"I find," said Calhoun, "that all I need is power. You drained my overdrive charge when you snatched my ship out of overdrive. I've extra Duhanne cells, but one overdrive charge is a lot of power to lose."

"You'll get it back," growled Walker. "Then take the prisoner and our warning to Canis. Get them to surrender if you can."

Calhoun considered. Under his coat, Murgatroyd said *"Chee! Chee!"* in a tone of some indignation.

"Thinking of the way of my own father with me," said Calhoun wryly, "and accepting your story itself as quite true—how the devil can I make your children believe that this time you aren't bluffing? Haven't you bluffed before?"

"We've threatened," said Walker, his eyes blazing. "Yes. And we were too soft-hearted to carry out our threats. We've tried everything short of force. But the time has come when we have to be ruthless! We have our wives to consider."

"Whom," observed Calhoun, "I suspect you didn't dare have with you because they wouldn't let you actually fight, no matter what your sons and daughters did."

"But they're not here now!" raged Walker. "And nothing will stop us!"

Calhoun nodded. In view of the situation as a whole, he almost believed it of the fathers of the colonists on

Canis III. But he wouldn't have believed it of his own father, regardless, and he did not think the young people of Canis would believe it of theirs. Yet there was nothing else for them to do.

It looked like he'd traveled three months in overdrive and painstakingly studied much distressing information about the ancestors of modern men, only to arrive at and witness the most heart-rending conflict in human history.

III.

"The fact that one statement agrees with another statement does not mean that both must be true. Too close an agreement may be proof that both statements are false. Conversely, conflicting statements may tend to prove each other's verity, if the conflict is in their interpretations of the facts they narrate . . ."

Manual, Interstellar Medical Service. P. 43.

They brought the prisoner a bare hour later. Sturdy, grizzled men had strung a line to the Med Ship's power bank, and there was that small humming sound which nobody quite understands as power flowed into the Duhanne cells. The power men regarded the inside of the ship without curiosity, as if too much absorbed in private bitterness to be interested in anything else. When they had gone, a small guard brought the prisoner. Calhoun noted the expression on the faces of these men, too. They hated their prisoner. But their faces showed the deep and wrenching bitterness a man does feel when his children have abandoned him for companions he considers worthless or worse. A man hates those companions corrosively, and these men hated their prisoner. But they could not help knowing that he, also, had abandoned some other father whose feelings were like their own. So there was frustration even in their fury.

The prisoner came lightly up the ladder into the Med

Ship. He was a very young man, with a singularly fair complexion and a carriage at once challengingly jaunty and defiant. Calhoun estimated his age as seven years less than his own, and immediately considered him irritatingly callow and immature because of it.

"You're my jailer, eh?" said the prisoner brightly, as he entered the Med Ship's cabin. "Or is this some new trick? They say they're sending me back. I doubt it!"

"It's true enough," said Calhoun. "Will you dog the airlock door, please? Do that and we'll take off."

The young man looked at him brightly. He grinned. "No," he said happily. "I won't."

Calhoun felt ignoble rage. There had been no great purpose in his request. There could be none in the refusal. So he took the prisoner by the collar and walked him into the airlock.

"We are going to be lifted soon," he said gently. "If the outer door isn't dogged, the air will escape from the lock. When it does, you will die. I can't save you, because if the outer door isn't dogged, all the air in the ship will go if I should try to help you. Therefore I advise you to dog the door."

He closed the inner door. He looked sick. Murgatroyd looked alarmedly at him.

"If I have to deal with that kind," Calhoun told the *tormal*, "I have to have some evidence that I mean what I say. If I don't, they'll be classing me with their fathers!"

The Med Ship stirred. Calhoun glanced at the external-field dial. The mobile landing grid was locking its force-field on. The little ship lifted. It went up and up and up. Calhoun looked sicker. The air in the lock was thinning swiftly. Two miles high. Three—

There were frantic metallic clankings. The indicator said that the outer door was dogged tight. Calhoun opened the inner door. The young man stumbled in, shockingly white and gasping for breath.

"Thanks," said Calhoun curtly.

He strapped himself in the control-chair. The vision-screens showed half the universe pure darkness and the rest a blaze of many-colored specks of light. They showed new stars appearing at the edge of the monstrous blackness. The Med Ship was rising ever more swiftly. Presently the black area was not half the universe. It was a third. Then a fifth. A tenth. It was a disk of pure darkness in a glory of a myriad distant sun.

The external-field indicator dropped abruptly to zero. The Med Ship was afloat in clear space. Calhoun tried the Lawlor drive, tentatively. It worked. The Med Ship swung in a vast curved course out of the dark planet's shadow. There was the sun Canis, flaming in space. Calhoun made brisk observations, set a new course, and the ship sped on with an unfelt acceleration. This was, of course, the Lawlor propulsion system, used for distances which were mere millions of miles.

When the ship was entirely on automatic control, Calhoun swung around to his unwilling companion. Murgatroyd was regarding the youthful stranger with intense curiosity. He looked at Calhoun with some apprehension.

"My name's Calhoun," Calhoun told him. "I'm Med Service. That's Murgatroyd. He's a *tormal*. Who are you and how did you get captured?"

The prisoner went instantly into a pose of jaunty defiance.

"My name is Fredericks," he said blandly. "What happens next?"

"I'm headed for Canis III," said Calhoun. "In part to land you. In part to try to do something about this war. How'd you get captured?"

"They made a raid," said young Fredericks scornfully. "They landed a rocket out in open country. We thought it was another propaganda bomb, like they've landed before—telling us we were scoundrels and such bilge. I went to see if there was anything in it good for a laugh. But it was bigger than usual. I didn't know, but men had

28

landed in it. They jumped me. Two of them. Piled me in the rocket and it took off. Then we were picked up and brought where you landed. They tried to mind-launder me!" He laughed derisively. "Showing me science stuff proving Phaedra's sun was going to blow and cook the old home planet. Lecturing me that we were all fools on Canis, undutiful sons and so on. Saying that to kill our parents wouldn't pay."

"Would it?" asked Calhoun. "Pay, that is?"

Fredericks grinned in a superior manner.

"You're pulling more of it, huh? I don't know science, but I know they've been lying to us! Look! They sent the first gang to Canis five years ago. Didn't send equipment with them, no more than they had to. Packed the ships full of people. They were twenty years old and so on. They had to sweat! Had to sweat out ores and make equipment and try to build shelters and plant food. There were more of them arriving all the time—shipped away from Phaedra with starvation rations so more of them could be shipped. All young people, remember! They had to sweat to keep from starving, with all the new ones coming all the time. Everybody had to pitch in the minute they got there. You never heard that, did you?"

"Yes," said Calhoun.

"They worked plenty!" said Fredericks scornfully. "Good little girls and boys! When they got nearly caught up, and figured that maybe in another month they could breathe easy, why then the old folks on Phaedra began to ship younger kids. Me among 'em! I was fifteen, and we hit Canis like a flood. There wasn't shelter, or food, or clothes to spare, but they had to feed us. So we had to help by working. And I worked! I built houses and graded streets and wrestled pipe for plumbing and sewage—the older boys were making it—and I planted ground and I chopped trees. No loafing! No fun! They piled us on Canis so fast it was root hog or die. And we rooted! Then just when we began to think that we could begin to take a breather they started dumping little kids

29

on us! Ten-year-olds and nine-year-olds to be fed and watched. Seven-year-olds to have their noses wiped! No fun, no rest—"

He made an angry, spitting noise.

"Did they tell you that?" he demanded.

"Yes," agreed Calhoun. "I heard that and more."

"All the time," raged Fredericks sullenly, "they were yelling at us that the sun back home was swelling. It was wobbling. It was throbbing like it was going to burst any minute! They kept us scared that any second the ships'd stop coming because there wasn't any more Phaedra. And we were good little boys and girls and we worked like hell. We tried to build what the kids they sent us needed, and they kept sending younger and younger kids. We got to the crack-up point. We couldn't keep it up! Night, day, every day, no fun, no loafing, nothing to do but work till you dropped, and then get up and work till you dropped again."

He stopped. Calhoun said:

"So you stopped believing it could be that urgent. You sent some messengers back to check and see. And Phaedra's sun looked perfectly normal, to them. There was no visible danger. The older people showed their scientific records, and your messengers didn't believe them. They decided they were faked. They were tired. All of you were tired. Young people need fun. You weren't having it. So when your messengers came back and said the emergency was a lie—you believed them. You believed the older people were simply dumping all their burdens on you, by lies."

"We knew it!" rasped Fredericks. "So we quit! We'd done our stuff! We were going to take time out and do some living! We were away back on having fun! We were away back on rest! We were away back just on shooting the breeze! We were behind on everything! We'd been slaves, following blueprints, digging holes and filling them up again." He stopped. "When they said all the old folks were going to move in on us, that was the finish! We're human! We've got a right to live like humans! When it came to building more houses and planting more land so more people—and old people at that——could move in to take over bossing us some more, we'd had it! We hadn't gotten anything out of the job for ourselves. If the old folks moved in, we never would! They didn't mind working us to death! To hell with them!"

"The reaction," said Calhoun, "was normal. But if one assumption was mistaken, it could still be wrong."

"What could be wrong?" demanded Fredericks angrily.

"The assumption that they lied," said Calhoun. "Maybe Phaedra's sun is getting ready to flare. Maybe your messengers were mistaken. Maybe you were told the truth."

Fredericks spat. Calhoun said:

"Will you clean that up, please?"

Fredericks gaped at him.

"Mop," said Calhoun. He gestured.

Fredericks sneered. Calhoun waited. Murgatroyd said agitatedly:

"Chee! Chee! Chee!"

Calhoun did not move. After a long time, Fredericks took the mop and pushed it negligently over the place he'd spat on.

"Thanks," said Calhoun.

He turned back to the control board. He checked his course and referred to the half-century-old Survey report on the Canis solar system. He scowled. Presently he said over his shoulder:

"How has the resting worked? Does everybody feel better?"

"Enough better," said Fredericks ominously, "so we're going to keep things the way they are! The old folks sent in a ship for a landing and we took the landing grid and dumped rocks where it'd run into them. We're going to set up little grids all over, so we can fling bombs up— we make good bombs—if they try to land anywhere besides Canopolis. And if they do make a landing, they'll

31

wish they hadn't! All they've dared so far is drop printed stuff calling us names and saying we've got to do what they say!"

Calhoun had the inner planet, Canis III, firmly in the center of his forward screen. He said negligently:

"How about the little kids? Most of you have quit work, you say—"

"There's not much work," bragged Fredericks. "We had to make stuff automatic as we built it, so we could all keep on making more things and not lose hands tending stuff we'd made. We got the designs from home. We do all right without working much!"

Calhoun reflected. If it were possible for any society to exist without private property, it would be this society, composed exclusively of the young. They do not want money as such. They want what it buys—now. There would be no capitalists in a world populated only by the younger generation from Phaedra. It would be an interesting sort of society, but thought for the future would be markedly lacking.

"But," said Calhoun, "what about the small children? The ones who need to be taken care of? You haven't got anything automatic to take care of them?"

"Pretty near!" Fredericks boasted. "Some of the girls like tending kids. Homely girls, mostly. But there's too many little ones. So we hooked up a psych circuit with multiple outlets for them. Some of the girls play with a couple of the kids, and that keeps the others satisfied. There was somebody studying pre-psych on Phaedra, and he was sent off with the rest to dig holes and build houses. He fixed up that trick so the girl he liked would be willing to take time off from tending kids. There's plenty of good technicians on Canis III! We can make out!"

There were evidently some very good technicians. But Calhoun began to feel sick. A psych circuit, of course, was not in itself a harmful device. It was a part of individual psychiatric equipment—not Med Service work—and its value was proved. In clinical use it permitted a psychiatrist to share the consciousness of his patient during interviews. He no longer had painfully to interpret his patient's thought-processes by what he said. He could observe the thought-processes themselves. He could trace the blocks, the mental sore spots, the ugly, not-human urges which can become obsessions.

Yes. A psych circuit was an admirable device in itself. But it was not a good thing to use for baby-tending.

There would be a great room in which hundreds of small children would sit raptly with psych-circuit receptors on their heads. They would sit quietly—very quietly—giggling to themselves, or murmuring. They would be having a very wonderful time. Nearby there would be a smaller room in which one or two other children played. There would be older girls to help these few children actually play. With what they considered adult attention every second, and with deep affection for their self-appointed nurses—why the children who actually played would have the very perfection of childhood pleasure. And their experience would be shared by—would simultaneously be known and felt by—would be the conscious and complete experience of each of the hundreds of other children tuned in on it by psych circuit. Each would feel every thrill and sensation of those who truly thrilled and experienced.

But the children so kept happy would not be kept exercised, nor stimulated to act, or think, or react for themselves. The effect of psych-circuit child-care would be that of drugs for keeping children from needing attention. The merely receiving children would lose all initiative, all purpose, all energy. They would come to wait for somebody else to play for them. And the death rate among them would be high and the health rate among those who lived would be low, and the injury to their personalities would be permanent if they played by proxy long enough.

And there was another uglier thought. In a society such as must exist on Canis III, there would be adolescents and post-adolescents who could secure incredible, fascinating pleasures for themselves—once they realized what could be done with a psych circuit.

Calhoun said evenly:

"In thirty minutes or so you can call Canopolis on space phone. I'd like you to call ahead. Will there be anybody on duty at the grid?"

Fredericks said negligently:

"There's usually somebody hanging out there. It makes a good club. But they're always hoping the old folks will try something. If they do—there's the grid to take care of them!"

"We're landing with or without help," said Calhoun. "But if you don't call ahead and convince somebody that one of their own is returning from the wars, they might take care of us with the landing grid."

Fredericks kept his jaunty air.

"What'll I say about you?"

"This is a Med Ship," said Calhoun with precision. "According to the Interstellar Treaty Organization agreement every planet's population can determine its government. Every planet is necessarily independent. I have nothing to do with who runs things, or who they trade or communicate with. I have nothing to do with anything but public health. But they'll have heard about Med Ships. You had, hadn't you?"

"Y—yes," agreed Fredericks. "When I went to school. Before I was shipped off to here."

"Right," said Calhoun. "So you can figure out what to say."

He turned back to the control board, watching the steadily swelling gibbous disk of the planet as the Med Ship drew near. Presently he reached out and cut the drive. He switched on the spacephone.

"Go ahead," he said dryly. "Talk us down or into trouble, just as you please."

34

IV.

"Experience directs that any assurance, at any time, that there is nothing wrong or that everything is all right, be regarded with suspicion. Certainly doctors often encounter patients who are ignorant of the nature of their trouble and its cause, and in addition have had their symptoms appear so slowly and so gradually that they were never noticed and still are not realized . . ."
Manual, Interstellar Medical Service. P. 68.

It was a very singular society on Canis III. After long and markedly irrelevant argument by spacephone, the Med Ship went down to ground in the grip of the Canopolis landing grid. This was managed with a deftness amounting to artistry. Whoever handled the controls did so with that impassioned perfection with which a young man can handle a mechanism he understands and worships. But it did not follow that so accomplished an operator would think beyond the perfection of performance. He came out and grinned proudly at the Med Ship when it rested, light as a feather, on the clear, grassy space in the center of the city's landing grid. He was a gangling seventeen or eighteen.

A gang—not a guard—of similar age came swaggering to interview the two in the landed spacecraft. Fredericks named where he'd been working and what he'd been doing and how he'd been taken prisoner. Nobody bothered to check his statements. But his age was almost a guarantee that he belonged on Canis. When he began his experiences as a prisoner among their enemies, all pretense of suspicion dropped away. The gang at the spaceport interjected questions, and whooped at some of his answers, and slapped each other and themselves ecstatically when he related some of the things he'd said and done in enemy hands, and talked loudly and boastfully of what they would do if the old folks tried to carry out their threats. But Calhoun observed no real preparations beyond the perfect working condition of the grid itself. Still, that ought to defend the planet adequately—except against such a mobile spaceport as he'd been captured by, himself.

When they turned to him for added reasons to despise the older generation, Calhoun said coldly:

"If you ask me, they can take over any time they're willing to kill a few of you to clear the way. Certainly if the way you're running this particular job is a sample!"

They bristled. And Calhoun marveled at the tribal organization which had sprung up among them. What Fredericks had said in the ship began to fit neatly into place with what once had been pure anthropological theory. He'd had to learn it because a medical man must know more than diseases. He must also know the humans who have them. Oddments of culture-instinct theory popped into his memory and applied exactly to what he was discovering. The theory says that the tribal cultures from which even the most civilized social organisms stem —were not human inventions. The fundamental facts of human society exist because human instinct directs them, in exact parallel to the basic design of the social lives of ants and bees. It seemed to Calhoun that he was seeing, direct, the operation of pure instinct in the divisions of function in the society he had encountered.

Here, where a guard must be mounted against enemies, he found young warriors. They took the task because it was their instinct. It was an hereditary impulse for young men of their age to act as youthful warriors at a post of danger. There was nothing more important to them than prestige among their fellows. They did not want wisdom, or security, or families, or possessions. The instinct of their age-group directed them as specifically as successive generations of social insects are directed. They moved about in gangs. They boasted vaingloriously. They loafed conspicuously and they would take lunatic risks for no reason whatsoever.

But they would never build cities of themselves. That

was the impulse of older men. In particular, the warrior age-group would be capable of immense and admirable skill in handling anything which interested them, but they would never devise automatic devices to keep a city going with next to no attention. They simply would not think so far ahead. They would fight and they would quarrel and they would brag. But if this eccentric world had survived so far, it must have additional tribal structure—it must have some more dedicated leadership than these flamboyant young men who guarded inadequately and operated perfectly the mechanism of a spaceport facility they would never have built.

"I've got to talk to somebody higher up," said Calhoun irritably. "A chief, really—a boss. Your war with your parents isn't my affair. I'm here on Med Service business. I'm supposed to check the public health situation with the local authorities and exchange information with them. So far as I'm concerned, this is a routine job."

The statement was not altogether truthful. In a sense, preventing unnecessary deaths was routine, and in that meaning Calhoun had exactly the same purpose on Canis III as on any other planet to which he might be sent. But the health hazards here were not routine. A society is an organism. It is a whole. Instinct-theory says that it can only survive as a whole, which must be composed of such-and-such parts. This society had suffered trauma, from the predicted dissolution of Phaedra's sun. Very many lives would be lost, unnecessarily, unless the results of that traumatic experience could be healed. But Calhoun's obligation was not to be stated in such terms to these young men.

"Who is running things?" demanded Calhoun. "A man named Walker said his son was bossing things here. He was pretty bitter about it, too! Who's looking after the distribution of food, and who's assigning who to raise more, and who's seeing that the small children get fed and cared for?"

The spaceport gang looked blank. Then someone said negligently:

"We take turns getting stuff to eat, for ourselves. The ones who landed here first, mostly, go around yelling at everybody. Sometimes the things they want get done. But they're mostly married now. They live in a center over yonder."

He gestured. Calhoun accepted it as a directive.

"Can somebody take me there?" he asked.

Fredericks said grandly:

"I'll do it. Going that way, anyhow. Who's got a ground-car I can use? My girl'll be worrying about me. Been worrying because she didn't know the old folks took me prisoner."

His proposal to acquire a ground-car was greeted with derision. There were ground-cars, but those that did not need repairs were jealously reserved by individuals for themselves and their closest friends. There was squabbling. Presently a scowling young man agreed to deliver Calhoun to the general area in which the first-landed of the colonists—now grown grim and authoritative—made their homes. It was annoying to wait while so simple a matter was discussed so vociferously. By the time it was settled, Fredericks had gone off in disgust.

The scowling youth produced his ground-car. Calhoun got in. Murgatroyd, of course, was not left behind. And the car was magnificent in polish and performance. Lavish effort and real ability had gone into its grooming and adjustment. With a spinning of wheels, it shot into immediate high speed. The dark-browed younglings drove with hair-raising recklessness and expertness. He traversed the city in minutes, and at a speed which allowed Calhoun only glimpses. But he could see that it was almost unoccupied.

Canopolis had been built by the youth of Phaedra to the designs of their elders for the reception of immigrants from the mother planet. It had been put up in frantic haste and used only as a receiving-depot. It had

38

needed impassioned and dedicated labor, and sustained and exhausting concentration to get it and the rest of the colonial facilities built against a deadline of doom. But now its builders were fed up with it. It was practically empty. The last arrivals had scattered to places where food supplies were nearer and a more satisfactory way of life was possible. There were broken windows and spattered walls. There was untidiness everywhere. But there had been great pains taken in the building. Some partly-completed enterprises showed highly competent workmanship.

Then the city ended and was a giant pile of structures which fell swiftly behind. The highways were improvised. They could be made more perfect later. Across the horizon there were jerry-built villages—temporary by design, because there had been such desperate need for so many of them so soon.

The ground-car came to a stop with a screaming of brakes at the edge of such a jerry-built group of small houses. A woman ran to hiding. A man ran into view. Another, and another, and another. They came ominously toward the car.

"Hop out," said the scowling driver. He grinned faintly. "They don't want me here. But I stirred 'em up, eh?"

Calhoun stepped out of the ground-car. It whirled on one pair of wheels and sped back to the city, its driver turning to make a derisive gesture at the men who had appeared. They were still quite young men—younger than Calhoun. They looked at him steadily.

He growled to himself. Then he called:

"I'm looking for somebody named Walker. He's supposed to be top man here."

A tense young man said sardonically:

"I'm Walker. But I'm not tops. Where'd you come from? With a Med Service uniform and a *tormal* on your shoulder you're not one of us! Have you come to argue that we ought to give in to Phaedra?"

Calhoun snorted.

"I've a message that an attack from space is due in three days, but that's all from Phaedra. I'm a Med Service man. How's the health situation? How are you equipped for doctors and such? How about hospitals? How's the death rate?"

The younger Walker grinned savagely.

"This is a new colony. I doubt there are a hundred people on the planet over twenty-five. How many doctors would there be in a population like ours? I don't think there is a death rate. Do you know how we came to be here?"

"Your father told me," said Calhoun, "at the military base on the next planet out. They're getting ready for an attack—and they asked me to warn you about it. Three days from now."

Young Walker ground his teeth.

"They won't dare attack. We'll smash them if they do. They lied to us! Worked us to death—"

"And no death rate?" asked Calhoun.

The younger man knitted his brows.

"There's no use your arguing with us. This is our world! We made it and we're keeping it! They made fools of us long enough!"

"And you've no health problems at all?"

The sardonic young man hesitated. One of the others said coldly:

"Make him happy. Let him talk to the women. They're worried about some of the kids."

Calhoun breathed a private sigh of relief. These relatively mature young men were the first-landed colonists. They'd had the hardest of all the tasks put upon the younger generation by the adults of Phaedra. They'd had the most back-breaking labor and the most urgent responsibilities. They'd been worked and stressed to the breaking-point. They'd finally arrived at a decision of desperation.

But apparently things could be worse. It is the custom, everywhere, for women to make themselves into whatever is most attractive to men. Young girls, in particular, will adopt any tradition which is approved of by their prospective husbands. And in a society to be formed brand-new, appalling new traditions could be started. But they hadn't. Deep-rooted instincts still worked. Women—young women—and girls appeared still to feel concern for young children which were not even their own. And Fredericks' story—

"By all means," agreed Calhoun. "If there's something wrong with the health of children—"

Young Walker gestured and turned back toward the houses. He scowled as he walked. Presently he said defensively:

"You probably noticed there aren't many people in the city."

"Yes," said Calhoun. "I noticed."

"We're not fully organized yet," said Walker, more defensively still. "We weren't doing anything but building. We've got to get organized before we'll have a regular economic system. Some of the later-comers don't know anything but building. When they're ready for it, the city will be occupied. We'll have as sound a system for production and distribution of goods as anywhere else. But we've just finished a revolution. In a sense we're still in it. But presently this world will be pretty much like any other—only better."

"I see," said Calhoun.

"Most people live in the little settlements, like this—close to the crops we grow. People raise their own food, and so on. In a way you may think we're primitive, but we've got some good technicians! When they get over not having to work for the old folks and finish making things just for themselves—we'll do all right. After all, we weren't trained to make a complete world. Just to make a world for the older people on Phaedra to take over! But we've taken it over for ourselves!"

"Yes," agreed Calhoun politely.

"We'll work out the other things," said young Walker truculently. "We'll have money, and credit, and hiring each other and so on. Right now defending ourselves is the top thing in everybody's mind."

"Yes," agreed Calhoun again. He was regarded as not quite an enemy, but he was not accepted as wholly neutral.

"The older ones of us are married," Walker said firmly, "and we feel responsibility, and we're keeping things pretty well in line. We were lied to, though, and we resent it. And we aren't letting in the old people to try to run us, when we've proved we can make and run a world ourselves!"

Calhoun said nothing. They reached a house. Walker turned to enter it, with a gesture for Calhoun to accompany him. Calhoun halted.

"Just a moment. The person who drove me here—when he turned up, at least one woman ran away and you men came out . . . well . . . pretty pugnaciously."

Walker flushed angrily.

"I said we had technicians. Some of them made a gadget to help take care of the children. That's harmless. But they want to use it to . . . to spy on older people with it. On us! Invasion of privacy. We don't like . . . well . . . they try to set up psych circuits near our homes. They . . . think it's fun to . . . know what people say and do—"

"Psych circuits can be useful," observed Calhoun, "or they can be pretty monstrous. On the other hand—"

"No decent man would do it!" snapped young Walker. "And no girl would have anything to do with anybody— But there are some crazy fools—"

"You have described," said Calhoun dryly, " a criminal class. Only instead of stealing other people's possessions they want to steal their sensations. Peeping-Tom stuff, eavesdropping on what other people feel about those they care for, as well as what they do and say. In a way it's a delinquency problem, isn't it?"

"There can't be a civilization without problems," said Walker. "But we're going to—" He opened a door. "My wife works with the kids the old people dumped on us. This way."

He motioned Calhoun inside the house. It was one of the shelters built during the frenzied building program designed to make an emergency refuge for the population of a planet. It was the roughest of machine-tool constructions. The floors were not finished. The walls were not smooth. The equipment showed. But there had been attempts to do something about the crudity. Colors had been used to try to make it homelike.

When a girl came in from the next room, Calhoun understood completely. She was a little younger than her husband, but not much. She regarded Calhoun with that anxiety with which a housekeeper always regards an unexpected visitor, hoping he will not notice defects. This young wife had those feminine instincts which are much older than tradition. Obligations and loyalties may be thrown aside, but a housewife's idea of her role is unchangeable.

"This is a Med Service man," said Walker briefly, indicating Calhoun. "I told him there was a health problem about some of the children." To Calhoun he said curtly: "This is my wife Elsa."

Murgatroyd said "*Chee!*" from where he clung to Calhoun's neck. He was suddenly reassured. He scrambled down to the floor. Elsa smiled at him.

"He's tame!" she said delightedly. "Maybe—"

Calhoun extended his hand. She took it. Murgatroyd, swaggering, extended his own black paw. Instead of conflict and hatred, here, Murgatroyd seemed to sense an amiable sociability such as he was used to. He felt more at home. He began zestfully to act like the human being he liked to pretend he was.

"He's delightful!" said the girl. "May I show him to Jak?"

Young Walker said:

"Elsa's been helping with the smaller kids. She says there's something the matter that she doesn't understand. She has one of the kids here. Bring him, Elsa."

She vanished. A moment later she brought in a small boy. He was probably six or seven. She carried him. He was thin. His eyes were bright, but he was completely passive in her arms. She put him down in a chair and he looked about alertly enough, but he simply did not move. He saw Murgatroyd, and beamed. Murgatroyd went over to the human who was near his own size. Swaggering, he offered his paw once more. The boy giggled, but his hand lay in his lap.

"He doesn't do anything!" said Elsa distressedly. "His muscles work, but he doesn't work them! He just sits and waits for things to be done for him! He acts as if he'd lost the idea of moving, or doing anything at all! And—it's beginning to show up among the other children! They just sit! They're bright enough . . . they see and understand—but they just sit!"

Calhoun examined the boy. His expression grew carefully impassive. But he winced as he touched the pipe-stem arms and legs. What muscles were there were almost like dough.

When he straightened up, despite himself his mouth was awry. Young Walker's wife said anxiously:

"Do you know what's the matter with him?"

"Basically," said Calhoun with a sort of desperate irony, "he's in revolt. As the rest of you are in revolt against Phaedra, he's in revolt against you. You needed rest you didn't get and recreation you couldn't have and something besides back-breaking labor under a load that grew heavier minute by minute for years. You revolted, and you've a fine justification for the war in which you're engaged. But he has needed something he hasn't had, too. So he's revolting against his lack—as you did—

and he's dying as you will presently do from exactly the same final cause."

Walker frowned ominously.

"I don't understand what you're saying!" he said harshly.

Calhoun moistened his lips.

"I spoke unprofessionally. The real cause of his present troubles and your future ones is that a social system has been shattered. The pieces can't live by themselves. And I don't know what medical measures can be taken to cure an injured civilization. As a medical man, I may be whipped. But I'd better check—Did I say, by the way, that the war fleet from Phaedra is going to attack in just three days?"

V.

". . . Truth is the accord of an idea with a thing. Very often an individual fails to discover the truth about some matter because he neglects to become informed about something. But even more often, the truth is never found out because somebody refuses to entertain an idea . . ."

Manual, Interstellar Medical Service. Pp. 101-2.

On the first day, Calhoun went grimly to the *creches* that had been set up by the first-arrived young colonists when ships began to discharge really young children at the landing grid in Canopolis. The *creches* were not too much like orphanages, of course, but the younger generation of Phaedra had been put in a very rough situation by the adults. If the time of the imminent solar explosion had been known, the matter could have been better handled. Actually, the explosion had been delayed—to date—for nearly five years from the discovery that it must occur. If that much leeway could have been predicted, older men and many machines would have been sent at first. But the bursting could not be computed. It was a matter of probability. Such-and-such unrhythmic variables must inevitably coincide sooner or later. When they did—final and ultimate catastrophe. The sun would flare terribly and destroy all life in its solar system. It could be calculated that the odds were even that the explosion would happen within one year, two to one within two, and five to one within three. The odds were enormous against Phaedra surviving as long as it had. The people of the mother-world had had a highly improbable break.

But in cold common sense they'd done the sensible thing. They'd tried to save those of their children who could take care of themselves first, and added others as they dared. But the burden on the young colonists had been monstrous. Even adults would have tended to grow warped with such pressure to mine, build, plough, and sow, as was put upon the youngsters. There had never been more than barely enough of food—and more mouths were always on the way. There had never been extra shelter, and younger and ever younger cargoes were constantly arriving, each needing more of shelter and of care than the ones before. And there was the world of adults still to be provided for.

Calhoun met the girls who had devoted themselves to the quasi-orphaned children. They bore themselves with rather touching airs of authority among the smaller children. But they were capable of ferocity, on occasion. They had the need, sometimes, not to defend their charges but themselves against the clumsily romantic advances of loutish teen-agers who considered themselves fascinating.

They had done very well.

The small children were exactly what Calhoun had anticipated—in every way. The small boy Calhoun had seen first was an extreme case, but the results of play by proxy were visible everywhere. Calhoun constrainedly inspected one after another of the children shelters. He was anxiously watched by the sober young faces of the nurses. But they giggled when Murgatroyd tried to go through Calhoun's actions of taking temperatures and the like. He had to be stopped when he attempted to take a throat-swabbing which Calhoun had said was pure routine.

After the fourth such inspection he said to Elsa:

"I don't need to see any more. What's happened to the boys the same age as these girl nurses—the thirteen and fourteen and fifteen-year-olds?"

Elsa said uncomfortably:

"They're mostly off in the wilds. They hunt and fish and pioneer. They don't care about girls. Some of them grow things . . . I don't think there'd be enough food if they didn't, even though we're not getting anybody new to feed."

Calhoun nodded. In all the cities of the galaxy, small children of both sexes were to be seen everywhere, and girls of the early teen-ages, and adults. But the boys' age-group he'd mentioned always made itself invisible. It congregated in groups away from the public eye, and engaged in adventurous games and quite futile explorations. It was socially quite self-sufficient everywhere.

"Your husband," said Calhoun, carefully impassive, "had better try to gather in some of them. As I remember it, they're capable of a rather admirable romantic idea of duty—for a while. We're going to need some romanticists presently."

Elsa had faith in Calhoun now, because he seemed concerned about the children. She said unhappily:

"Do you really think the . . . old people will attack? I've grown older since I've been here. Those of us who came first are almost like the people on Phaedra—some ways. The younger people are inclined to be suspicious of us because we . . . try to guide them."

"If you're confiding that you think there may be two sides to this war," Calhoun told her, "you are quite right. But see what your husband can do about gathering some of the hunting-and-fishing members of the community. I've got to get back to my ship."

He got himself driven back to the landing grid. Walker did not drive him, but another of the now-suspect men of twenty-five or so, from the shelter village of the first-landed colonists. He was one of those who'd worked with Walker from the beginning and with him had been most embittered. Now he found himself almost a member of an older generation. He was still bitter against the people of Phaedra, but—

"This whole business is a mess!" he said darkly as he drove through the nearly deserted city toward the landing grid. "We've got to figure out a way to organize things that'll be better than the old way. But no organization at all is no good, either! We've got some tough young characters who like it this way, but they've got to be tamed down!"

Calhoun had his own unsettling suspicions. There have always been splendid ideas of social systems which will make earthly paradises for their inhabitants. Here, by happenchance, there had come to be a world inhabited only by the young. He tried to put aside, for the moment, what he was unhappily sure he'd find out back at the ship. He tried to think about this seemingly perfect opportunity for a new and better organization of human lives.

But he couldn't believe in it. Culture-instinct theory is pretty well worked out. The Med Service considered it proven that the basic pattern of human societies is instinctual rather than evolved by trial and error. The individual human being passes through a series of instinct-patterns which fit him at different times to perform different functions in a social organization which can vary but never change its kind. It has to make use of the successive functions its members are driven by instinct to perform. If it does not use its members, or give scope to their instincts, it cannot survive. The more lethal attempts at novel societies tried not only to make all their members alike, but tried to make them all alike at all ages. Which could not work.

Calhoun thought unhappily of the tests he meant to make in the Med Ship. As the ground-car swerved into the great open center of the grid, he said:

"My job is doing Med Service. I can't advise you how to plan a new world. If I could, I wouldn't. But whoever does have authority here had better think about some very immediate troubles."

"We'll fight if Phaedra attacks!" said the driver darkly. "They'll never get to ground alive, and if they do—they'll wish they hadn't!"

"I wasn't thinking of Phaedra," said Calhoun.

The car stopped close by the Med Ship. He got out. There had been attempts to enter the ship in his absence. The gang which occupied the control building and in theory protected Canis III against attack from the sky had tried to satisfy their curiosity about the little ship. They'd even used torches on the metal. But they hadn't gotten in.

Calhoun did. Murgatroyd chattered shrilly when he was put down. He scampered relievedly about the cabin, plainly rejoicing at being once more in familiar surroundings. Calhoun paid no attention. He closed and dogged the air-lock door. He switched on the spacephone and said shortly:

"Med Ship *Esclipus Twenty* calling Phaedrian fleet. Med Ship *Esclipus Twenty* calling—"

The loud-speaker fairly deafened him as somebody yelled into another spacephone mike in the grid-control building.

"*Hey! You in the ship! Stop that! No talking with the enemy!*"

Calhoun turned down the incoming volume and said patiently:

"Med Ship *Esclipus Twenty* calling fleet from Phaedra.

49

Come in, fleet from Phaedra! Med Ship *Esclipus Twenty* calling—"

There was a chorus of yelling from the nearby building. The motley, swaggering, self-appointed landing-grid guard had tried to break into the ship out of curiosity, but they were vastly indignant when Calhoun did something of which they disapproved. They made it impossible for him to have heard a reply from the space fleet presumably overhead. But after a moment someone in the control house evidently elbowed the others aside and shouted:

"You! Keep that up and we'll smash you! We've got the grid to do it with, too!"

Calhoun said curtly:

"Med Ship to Control. I've something to tell you. Suppose you listen. But not on spacephone. Have your best grid technician come outside and then I shall tell him by speaker."

He snapped off the spacephone and watched. The control building fairly erupted indignant youths. After a moment he saw the gangling one who'd grinned so proudly when the Med Ship was landed with absolute perfection. The others shouted and scowled at the ship.

Calhoun threw on the outside speaker—normally used for communication with a ground crew before lifting.

"I'm set," said Calhoun coldly, "for overdrive travel. My Duhanne cells are charged to the limit. If you try to form a force-field around this ship, I'll dump half a dozen overdrive charges into it in one jolt that will blow every coil you've got! And then how'll you fight the ships from Phaedra? I'm going to talk to them on spacephone. Listen in if you like. Monitor it. But don't try to bother me!"

He threw on the spacephone again and patiently resumed his calling:

"Med Ship *Esclipus Twenty* calling fleet from Phaedra! Med Ship calling fleet from Phaedra—"

He saw violent argument outside the grid's control

building. Some of the young figures raged. But the youth who'd handled the grid so professionally raged at them. Calhoun hadn't made an idle threat. A grid-field could be blown out. A grid could be made useless by one of the ships it handled. When a ship like Calhoun's went into overdrive, it put out something like four ounces of pure energy to form a field in which it could travel past the speed of light. In terms of horsepower or kilowatt hours, so much force would be meaningless. It was too big. It was a quantity of energy whose mass was close to four ounces. When the ship broke out of overdrive, that power was largely returned to storage. The loss was negligible, compared to the total. But, turned loose into a grid's force-field, even three or four such charges would work havoc with the grid's equipment.

Calhoun got an answer from emptiness just as the members of the group by the control building shouted each other down and went inside to listen with bitter unease and suspicion to his talk with the enemy.

"*Phaedra fleet calling,*" said a growling voice in the spacephone speaker. "*What do you want?*"

"To exercise my authority as a Med Service officer," said Calhoun heavily. "I warn you that I now declare this planet under quarantine. All contact with it from space is forbidden until health hazards here are under control. You will inform all other spacecraft and any other spaceport you may contact of this quarantine. Message ends."

Silence. A long silence. The growling voice rasped: "*What's that? Repeat it!*"

Calhoun repeated it. He switched off the phone and unpacked the throat-swabbings he'd made at the four children's shelters in turn. He opened up his laboratory equipment. He put a dilution of one throat-swabbing into a culture slide that allowed living organisms to be examined as they multiplied. He began to check his highly specific suspicions. Presently he was testing them

51

with minute traces of various antibodies. He made rough but reasonably certain identifications. His expression grew very, very sober. He took another swab sample and put it through the same process. A third, and fourth, and fifth, and tenth. He looked very grim.

It was sunset outside when there was a hammering on the ship's hull. He switched on a microphone and speaker.

"What do you want?" he asked flatly.

The angry voice of young Walker came from the gathering darkness. The screens showed a dozen or more inhabitants of Canis III milling angrily about him. Some were of the young-warrior age. They engaged in bitter argument. But the younger Walker, and four or five with him, faced the ship with ominous quietness.

"What's this nonsense about quarantine?" demanded Walker harshly, from outside. "Not that we've space-commerce to lose, but what does it mean?"

"It means," Calhoun told him, "that your brave new world rates as a slum. You've kept kids quiet with psych circuits, and they haven't eaten properly and haven't exercised at all. They're weak from malnutrition and feeble from not doing their own playing. They're like slum children used to be in past ages. Here on Canis you're about ready to wipe yourselves out. You may have done it."

"You're crazy!" snapped Walker. But he was upset.

"In the four shelters I visited," Calhoun said drearily. "I spotted four cases of early diphtheria, two of typhoid, three of scarlet fever and measles, and samples of nearly any other disease you care to name. The kids have been developing those diseases out of weakness and from the reservoir of infections we humans always carry with us. They'd reached the contagious stage before I saw them —but all the kids are kept so quiet that nobody noticed that they were sick. They've certainly spread to each other and their nurses, and therefore out into your general population, all the infections needed for a first-rate multiple epidemic. And you've no doctors, no anti-biotics—not even injectors to administer shots with if you had them."

"*You're crazy!*" cried young Walker. "*Crazy! Isn't this a Phaedra trick to make us give in?*"

"Phaedra's trick," said Calhoun more drearily than before, "is an atom bomb they're going to drop into this landing grid—I suspect quarantine or no quarantine—in just two days more. Considering the total situation, I don't think that matters."

VI.

". . . The most difficult of enterprises is to secure the co-operation of others in enterprises those others did not think of first . . ."

Manual, Interstellar Medical Service. P. 189.

Calhoun worked all night, tending and inspecting the culture incubators which were part of the Med Ship's technical equipment. In the children's shelters, he'd swabbed throats. In the ship, he'd diluted the swabbings and examined them microscopically. He'd been depressingly assured of his very worst fears as a medical man—all of which could have been worked out in detail from the psych circuit system of child care boastfully described by Fredericks. He could have written out his present results in advance from a glance at the child Jak shown him by the younger Walker's wife. But he hated to find that objective information agreed with what he would have predicted by theory.

In every human body there are always germs. The process of good health is in part a continual combat with slight and unnoticed infections. Because of victories over small invasions, a human body acquires defenses against larger invasions of contagion. Without such constant small victories, a body ceases to keep its defenses strong against beachheads of infection. Yet malnutrition or even exhaustion can weaken a body once admirably equipped for this sort of guerilla warfare.

If an undernourished child fails to win one skirmish, he can become overwhelmed by a contagion the same child would never have known about had he only been a little stronger. But, overwhelmed, he is a sporadic case of disease—a case not traceable to another clinical case. And then he is the origin of an epidemic. In slum conditions a disease not known in years can arise and spread like wildfire. With the best of intentions and great technical ingenuity, the younger-generation colonists of Canis III had made that process inevitable among the younger children who were their last-imposed burden. The children were under-exercised, under-stimulated, and hence under par in appetite and nutrition. And it is an axiom of the Med Service that a single underfed child can endanger an entire planet.

Calhoun proved the fact with appalling certainty. His cultures astounded even him. But by dawn he had applied Murgatroyd's special genetic abilities to them. Murgatroyd said *"Chee!"* in a protesting tone when Calhoun did what was necessary at that small patch on his flank which was quite insensitive. But then Murgatroyd shook himself and admiringly scowled back at Calhoun, imitating the intent and worried air that Calhoun wore. Then he followed Calhoun about in high good spirits, strutting on his hind legs, man-fashion, and pretending to set out imaginary apparatus as Calhoun did, long ahead of time for what he hoped would occur.

Presently Murgatroyd tired—a little quicker than usual —and went to sleep. Calhoun bent over him and counted his respiration and heart beat. Murgatroyd slept on. Calhoun gnawed his fingers in anxious expectation.

He'd come on this assignment with some resentment because he thought it foolish. He'd carried on with increasing dismay as he found it not absurd. Now he watched over Murgatroyd with the emotional concern a medical man feels when lives depend upon his professional efficiency, but that efficiency depends on something beyond his control. Murgatroyd was that something this time—but there was one other.

The *tormal* was a pleasant little animal, and Calhoun liked him very much. But *tormals* were crew-members of one-man Med Ships because their metabolism was very similar to that of humans, but no *tormal* had ever been known to die of an infectious disease. They could play host to human infections, but only once and only lightly. It appeared that the furry little creatures had a hair-trigger sensitivity to bacterial toxins. The presence of infective material in their blood streams produced instant and violent reaction—and the production of antibodies in large quantity. Theorists said that *tormals* had dynamic immunity-systems instead of passive ones, like humans. Their body-chemistry seemed to look truculently for microscopic enemies to destroy, rather than to wait for something to develop before they fought it.

If he reacted normally, now, in a matter of hours his blood stream would be saturated with antibodies—or an antibody—lethal to the cultures Calhoun had injected. There was, however, one unfortunate fact. Murgatroyd weighed perhaps twenty pounds. There was most of a planetary population needing antibodies only he could produce.

He slept from breakfast-time to lunch. He breathed slightly faster than he should. His heart beat was troubled.

Calhoun swore a little when noon came. He looked at the equipment all laid out for biological mircroanalysis —tiny test tubes holding half a drop, reagent flasks dispensing fractions of milliliters, tools and scales much tinier than doll-size. If he could determine the structure and formula of an antibody—or antibodies—that Murgatroyd's tiny body formed—why synthesis in quantity should be possible. Only the Med Ship had not materials for so great an amount of product.

There was only one chance. Calhoun threw the space-phone switch. Instantly a voice came from the speaker.

". . . *ing Med Ship Esclipus Twenty! Phaedra fleet calling Med Ship Esclipus Twenty!*"

"Med Ship answering," said Calhoun. "What is it?"

The voice went on: "*Calling Med Ship Twenty! Calling Med Ship Esclipus Twenty! Calling—*" It went on interminably. It was a very long way off, if it took so long for Calhoun's answer to be heard. But the call-formula broke off. "*Med Ship! Our doctors want to know the trouble on Canis! Can we help? We've hospital ships equipped and ready!*"

"The question," said Calhoun steadily, "is whether I can make a formula-and-structure identification, and whether you can synthesize what I identify. How's your lab? How are you supplied with biological crudes?"

He waited. By the interval between his answer and a reply to it, the ship he'd communicated with was some five million miles or more away. But it was still not as far as the next outward planet where the Phaedrian fleet was based.

While he waited for his answer, Calhoun heard murmurings. They would come from the control building at the side of the grid. The loutish, suspicious gang there was listening. Calhoun had threatened to wreck the grid if they tried anything on the Med Ship—but he could do nothing unless they tried to use a force-field. They listened in, muttering among themselves.

A long time later the voice from space came back. The fleet of the older generation of Phaedra was grounded, save for observation ships like the one speaking. The fleet had full biological equipment for any emergency. It could synthesize any desired compound up to— The degree of complexity and the classification was satisfactory.

"Day before yesterday," said Calhoun, "when you had me aground on Canis IV, your leader Walker said your children on this planet were destroying your grandchildren. He didn't say how. But the process is well under way—only the whole population will probably go with them. Most of the population, anyhow. I'm going to need those hospital ships and your best biological chemists—I hope! Get them started this way—fast! I'll try to make a deal for at least the hospital ships to be allowed to land. Over."

He did not flick off the spacephone. He listened. And a bitter, envenomed voice came from nearby:

"Sure! Sure! We'll let 'em land ships they say are hospital ships, loaded down with men and guns! We'll land 'em ourselves, we will!"

There was a click. The spacephone in the control building was turned off.

Calhoun turned back to the sleeping Murgatroyd. There was a movement about the grid-control building. Sleek, glistening ground-cars hurtled away—two of them. Calhoun turned them to the planetary communicator. It could break in on any wave-length used for radio communication under a planet's Heaviside roof. He had to get in touch with Walker or some other of the first-landed colonists. They were still embittered against their home world, but they must be beginning to realize that Calhoun had told the truth about the youngest children. They'd find sickness if they looked for it.

But the planetary communicator picked up nothing. No radiation wave-length was in use. There was no organized news service. The young people on Canis III were too self-centered to care about news. There were no entertainment programs. Only show-offs would want to broadcast, and show-offs would not make the apparatus.

So Calhoun could not communicate save by spacephone, with a range of millions of miles, and the ship's exterior loud-speakers, with a range of hundreds of feet. If he left the Med Ship, he wasn't likely to be able to fight his way back in. He couldn't find the younger

Walker on foot, in any case, and he did not know anyone else to seek.

Besides, there was work to be done in the ship.

Before Murgatroyd waked, the two ground-cars had returned. At intervals, nearly a dozen other cars followed to the control building, hurtling across the grid's clear center with magnificent clouds of dust following them. They braked violently when they arrived. Youths piled out. Some of them yelled at the Med Ship and made threatening gestures. They swarmed into the building.

Murgatroyd said tentatively, "*Chee?*"

He was awake. Calhoun could have embraced him.

"Now we see what we see!" he said grimly. "I hope you've done your stuff, Murgatroyd!"

Murgatroyd came obligingly to him, and Calhoun lifted him to the table he had ready. Again, what he did did not hurt. A tiny patch on Murgatroyd's side had been made permanently insensitive shortly after he was born. Calhoun extracted a quantity of what he hoped was a highly concentrated bacterial antagonist. He took thirty CCs in all. He clumped the red cells. He separated the serum. He diluted an infinitesimal bit of it and with a steady hand added it to a slide of the same cultures—living—on which Murgatroyd's dynamic immunity system had worked.

The cultures died immediately.

Calhoun had an antibody sample which could end the intolerable now-spreading disaster on the world of young people—*if* he could analyze it swiftly and accurately, and *if* the hospital ships from Phaedra could be landed, and *if* they could synthesize some highly complex antibody compounds, and *if* the inhabitants of Canis III would lay aside their hatred—

He heard a tapping sound on the Med Ship's hull. He looked at a screen. Two youths stood in the doorway of the control building, leisurely shooting at the Med ship with sporting weapons.

58

Calhoun set to work. Sporting rifles were not apt to do much damage.

For an hour, while there was the occasional clanking of a missile against the ship's outer planking, he worked at the infinitely delicate job of separating serum from its antibody content. For another hour he tried to separate the antibody into fractions. Incredibly, it would not separate. It was one substance only.

There was a crackling sound and the whole ship shivered. The screen showed a cloud of smoke drifting away. The members of the grid-guard had detonated some explosive—intended for mining, most likely—against one of the landing-fins.

Calhoun swore. His call to the Phaedrian fleet was the cause. The grid-guard meant to allow no landing. He'd threatened to blow out their controls if they tried to use the grid on the Med Ship, but they wanted it ready for use as a weapon against the space fleet. They couldn't use it against him. He couldn't damage it unless they tried. They wanted him away.

He went back to his work. From time to time, annoyedly, he looked up at the outside. Presently a young-warrior group moved toward the ship, carrying something very heavy. A larger charge of explosive, perhaps.

He waited until they were within yards of the ship. He stabbed the emergency-rocket button. A thin, pencil-like rod of flame shot downward between the landing-fins. It was blue-white—the white of a sun's surface. For one instant it splashed out hungrily before it bored and melted a hole into the ground itself into which to flow. But in that instant it had ignited the covering of the burden the youths carried. They dropped it and fled. The pencil flame bored deeper and deeper into the ground. Clouds of smoke and steam arose.

There was a lurid flash. The burden that the young warriors had abandoned, vanished in a flare that looked like a lightning bolt. The ship quivered from the detonation. A crater appeared where the explosive had been.

Calhoun cut off the emergency rocket, which had burned for ten seconds at one-quarter thrust.

Sunset came and night fell for the second time. He noticed, abruptly, that some of the ground-cars from about the control building went racing away. But they did not pass close to the Med Ship in their departure. He labored on. He'd spent nearly thirty hours making cultures from the specimens swabbed from children's throats, and injecting Murgatroyd, and waiting for his reaction, and then separating a tiny quantity of anti-body—which would not total more than the dust from a butterfly's wing—from the serum he obtained.

Now he worked on, through the night. Far away—some tens or scores of millions of miles—the hospital ships of the Phaedrian fleet took off from the next out-ward planet. They would be coming at full speed toward Canis III. They would need the results of the work Calhoun was doing, if they were to prevent an appalling multiple plague which could wipe out all the sacrifice the building of the colony had entailed. But his work had to be exact.

It was tedious. It was exacting. It was exhaustingly time-consuming. He did have the help of previous experience, and the knowledge that the most probable molecular design would include this group of radicals and probably that, and side-chains like this might be looked for, and co-polymers might— But he was bleary-eyed and worn out before dawn came again. His eyes felt as if there were grains of sand beneath their lids. His brain felt dry—felt fibrous inside his skull, as if it were excelsior. But when the first red colors showed in the east, with the towers of the city against them, he had the blue-print of what should be the complex molecule formed in Murgatroyd's furry body.

He had just begun to realize, vaguely, that his work was done, when twin glaring lights came bouncing and plunging across the empty center of the grid. They were extraordinarily bright in the ruddy darkness. They stopped. A man jumped from the ground-car and ran toward the ship.

Calhoun wearily threw on the outer microphones and speakers.

"What's the matter now?" The man was the younger Walker.

"You're right!" called Walker's voice, strained to the breaking point. "There is sickness! Everywhere! There's an epidemic! It's just beginning! People felt tired and peevish and shut themselves away. Nobody realized! But they've got fevers! They're showing rashes! There's some delirium! The smallest children are worst—they were always quiet—but it's everywhere! We've never had real sickness before! What can we do?"

Calhoun said tiredly:

"I've got the design for an antibody. Murgatroyd made it. It's what he's for. The hospital ships from Phaedra are on the way now. They'll start turning it out in quantity and their doctors will start giving everybody shots of it."

Young Walker cried out fiercely:

"But that would mean they'd land! They'd take over! I can't let them land! I haven't the power! Nobody has! Too many of us would rather die than let them land! They lied to us. It's bad enough to have them hovering outside. If they land, there'll be fighting everywhere and forever! We can't let them help us! We won't! We'll fight—we'll die first!"

Calhoun blinked, owlishly.

"That," he said exhaustedly, "is something you have to figure out for yourself. If you're determined to die, I can't stop you. Die first or die second—it's your choice. You make it. I'm going to sleep!"

He cut off the mike and speakers. He couldn't keep his eyes open.

VII.

". . . As a strictly practical matter, a man who has to leave a task that he has finished, and wishes it to remain as he leaves it, usually finds it necessary to give the credit for his work to someone who will remain on the spot and will thereby be moved to protect and defend it so long as he lives . . ."

Manual, Interstellar Medical Service. Pp. 167-8.

Murgatroyd tugged at Calhoun and shrilled anxiously into his ear.

"Chee-chee!" he cried frantically. *"Chee-chee-chee!"*

Calhoun blinked open his eyes. There was a crashing sound and the Med Ship swayed upon its landing fins. It almost went over. It teetered horribly, and then slowly swung back past uprightness and tilted nearly as far in the opposite direction. There were crunching sounds as the soil partly gave way beneath one landing fin.

Then Calhoun waked thoroughly. In one movement he was up and launching himself across the cabin to the control-chair. There was another violent impact. He swept his hand across the row of studs which turned on all sources of information and communication. The screens came on, and the spacephone, and the outside mikes and loud-speakers, and even the planetary communication unit which would have reported had there been any use of the electromagnetic spectrum in the atmosphere of this planet.

Bedlam filled the cabin. From the spacephone speaker a stentorian voice shouted:

"This is our last word! Permit our landing or—"

A thunderous detonation was reported by the outside mikes. The Med ship fairly bounced. There was swirling white smoke outside the ship. It was mid-morning, now, and the giant lacy structure of the landing grid was silhouetted against a deep-blue sky. There were cracklings from some electric storm perhaps a thousand miles away. There were shoutings, also brought in by the outside mikes.

Two groups of figures, fifty or a hundred yards from the Med ship, labored furiously over some objects on the ground. Smoke billowed out; then a heavy, blastlike *"Boom!"* Something came spinning through the air, end over end, with sputtering sparks trailing behind it. It fell close by the base of the upright Med Ship.

Calhoun struck down the emergency rocket stud as it exploded. The roar of the rocket filled the interior of the ship. The spacephone speaker bellowed again:

"We've got a megaton bomb missile headed down! This is our last word! Permit landing or we come in fighting!"

The object from the crude cannon went off violently. With the emergency rocket flaming to help, it lifted the Med Ship, which jerked upward, settled back—and only two of its fins touched solidity. It began to topple because there was no support for the third.

Once toppled over, it would be helpless. It could be blasted with deliberately placed charges between its hull and the ground. A crater already existed where support for the third landing fin should have been.

Calhoun pushed the stud down full. The ship steadied and lifted. It went swinging across the level center of the landing grid. Its slender, ultra-high-velocity flame knifed down through the sod, leaving a smoking, incandescent slash behind. The figures about the bomb-throwers scattered and fled. The Med Ship straightened to an upright position and began to rise.

Calhoun swore. The grid was the planet's defense against landings from space, because it could fling out missiles of any size with perfect aim at any target within some hundred thousand miles—a good twelve planetary diameters. Its operators meant to defy the fleet from Phaedra and had to get rid of the Med Ship before they dared energize its coils. Now they were rid of it.

Now they could throw bombs, or boulders, or anything else its force-fields could handle.

The spacephone roared again:

"On the ground there! Our missile is aimed straight for your grid! It carries a megaton fission bomb! Evacuate the area!"

Calhoun swore again. The gang, the guard, the young-warrior group at the grid would be far too self-confident to heed such a threat. If there were wiser heads on Canis III, they could not enforce their commands. A human community has to be complete or it is not workable. The civilization which had existed on Phaedra II was shattered by the coming doom of its sun. The fragments—on Phaedra, in the fleet, in each small occupied community on Canis III—were incomplete and incapable of thinking or acting in concert with any other. Every small group on this planet, certainly, gave only lip-service to the rest. The young world was inherently incapable of organizing itself, save on a miniature scale. And one such miniature group had the grid and would fight with it regardless of the wishes of any other—because that group happened to be composed of instinct-driven members of the young-warrior group.

But he was still within the half-mile-high fence of the grid's steel structure. He strapped himself in his seat. The ship rose and rose. It came level with the top of the colony's one defense against space. The peculiar, corrugated copper lip of that structure, formed into the force-field guide which made it usable, swung toward him. He raised the rocket-thrust and shot skyward.

A deafening bellow came from the speakers:

"Yeah! Go on out and join the old folk! We'll get you!"

Obviously, the voice was from the ground below him. The ship flashed upward. Calhoun rasped into the spacephone mike, himself:

"Med Ship calling fleet! Call back that missile! I've

got the antibody structure! This is no time for fighting! Call your missile back!"

Derisive laughter—again from the ground. Then the heavy, growling voice of an older man.

"Keep out of the way, Med Ship! These young fools are destroying themselves. Now they're destroying our grandchildren! If we hadn't been soft-hearted before— if we'd fought them from the beginning—the little ones wouldn't be dying now! Keep out of the way! If you can help us, it'll be after we've won the war!"

The sky turned purple, at the height Calhoun had reached. It went black. The sun Canis flamed and flared against a background of ebony space, sprinkled with a thousand million colored stars. The Med Ship continued to rise.

Calhoun felt singularly and helplessly alone. Below him the sunlit surface of a world spread out, its edge already curving, cloud-masses in its atmosphere veiling the details of mountains and green-clad plains. There was the blue of ocean, creeping in. The city of the land-grid was tiny, now. The brown of ploughed fields was no longer divided into rectangular shapes. It was a mere brownish haze between the colorings of as-yet-untouched virgin areas. The colonists of Canis III had so far made only a part of the new world their own. Many times more remained to be turned to human use.

The rear screen showed something coming upward. Masses of stuff, without shape but with terrific velocity. It was inchoate, indefinite stuff. It was plain dirt from the center of the landing-grid's floor, flung upward with the horrible power available for the landing and launching of ships. And, focused upon it, the force-fields of the gird could control it absolutely for a hundred thousand miles.

Calhoun swerved, ever so slightly. His own velocity had reached miles per second, but the formless mass following him was traveling at tens. It would not matter what such a hurtling missile was. At such a velocity it would not strike like a mass, but like a meteor-shower, flaring into incandescence when it touched and vaporizing the Med Ship with itself in the flame of impact.

But the grid would have to let go before it hit. There was monstrous stored power in the ship's Duhanne cells. If so much raw energy were released into anything on which a force-field was focused, it would destroy the source of the field. The grid could control its battering-ram until the very last fraction of a second, but then it must release—and its operator knew it.

Calhoun swung his ship frantically.

The mass of speeding planet-matter raced past no more than hundreds of yards away. It was released. It would go on through empty space for months or years—perhaps forever.

Calhoun swung back to his upward course. Now he sent raging commands before him:

"Pull back that missile! You can't land a bomb on Canis! There are people there! You can't drop a bomb on Canis!"

There was no answer. He raged again:

"Med Ship calling Phaedra fleet! There's disease on Canis! Your children and grandchildren are stricken! You can't fight your way to help them! You can't blast your way to sickbeds! You've got to negotiate! You've got to compromise! You've got to make a bargain or you and they together—"

A snarling voice from the ground said spitefully:

"*Never mind little Med man! Let 'em try to land! Let 'em try to take over and boss us! We listened to them long enough! Let 'em try to land and see what happens! We've got their fleet spotted! We'll take care of them!*"

Then the growling tones Calhoun had come to associate with Phaedra:

"*You keep out of the way, Med Ship. If our young children are sick, we're going to them! We're just beyond the area in which no drive will work. When the grid has*

66

been blasted our landing ship will go down and we'll come in! Our missile is only half an hour from target now! We'll begin our landing in three hours or less! Out of the way!"

Calhoun said very bitter and extremely impolite words. But he faced an absolute emotional stalemate between enemies of whom both were in the wrong. The frantic anger of the adults of Phaedra, barred from the world to which they'd sent their children first so they could stay where doom awaited, was matched by the embittered revolt of the young people who had been worked past endurance and burdened past anyone's power to tolerate. There could be no compromise. It was not possible for either side to confess even partial defeat by the other. The quarrel had to be fought to a finish as between the opposing sides, and then hatred would remain no matter which side won. Such hatred could not be reasoned with.

It could only be replaced by a greater hatred.

Calhoun ground his teeth. The Med Ship hurtled out from the sunlit Canis III. Somewhere—not many thousands of miles away— the fleet of Phaedra clustered. Its crews were raging, but they were sick with anxiety about the enemies they prepared to fight. Aground there was hatred among the older of the colonists—the young-warrior group in particular, because that is the group in which hate is appropriate—and there was no less a sickish disturbance because even in being right they were wrong. Every decent impulse that had been played upon to make them exhaust themselves, before their revolt, now protested the consequences of their revolt. Yet they believed that in revolting they were justified.

Murgatroyd did not like the continued roar of emergency-rockets. He climbed up on Calhoun's lap and protested.

"*Chee!*" he said urgently. "*Chee-chee!*"

Calhoun grunted.

"Murgatroyd," he said, "it is a Med Service rule that a

67

Med Ship man is expendable in case of need. I'm very much afraid that we've got to be expended. Hang on, now! We try some action!"

He turned the Med Ship end for end and fed full power to the rockets. The ship would decelerate even faster than it had gathered speed. He set the nearest-object indicator to high gain. It showed the now-retreating mass of stone and soil from Canis. Calhoun then set up a scanner to examine a particular part of the sky.

"Since fathers can be insulted," he observed, "they've made a missile to fight its way down through anything that's thrown at it. It'll be remote-controlled for the purpose. It's very doubtful that there's a spaceship on the planet to fight it back. There's been no reference to one, anyhow. So what the missile will have to fight off will be stuff from the landing-grid only. Which is good. Moreover, fathers being what they are, regardless, that missile won't be a high-speed one. They'll want to be able to call it back at the last minute. They'll hope to."

"*Chee!*" said Murgatroyd, insisting that he didn't like the rocket-roar.

"So we will make ourselves as unpopular as possible with the fathers," observed Calhoun, "and if we live through it we will make ourselves even more cordially hated by the sons. And then they will be able to tolerate each other a little, because they both hate us so much. And so the public-health situation on Canis III may be resolved. Ah!"

The nearest-object indicator showed something moving toward the Med Ship. The scanner repeated the information in greater detail. There was a small object headed toward the planet from empty space. Its velocity and course—

Calhoun put on double acceleration to intercept it, while he pointed the ship quartering so he'd continue to lose outward speed.

Ten minutes later the spacephone growled:

"Med Ship! What do you think you're doing?"

"Getting in trouble," said Calhoun briefly.

Silence. The screens showed a tiny pin point of moving light, far away toward emptiness. Calhoun computed his course. He changed it.

"Med Ship!" rasped the spacephone. *"Keep out of the way of our missile! It's a megaton bomb!"*

Calhoun said irrelevantly:

"Those who in quarrels interpose, must often wipe a bloody nose." He added. "I know what it is."

"Let it alone!" rasped the voice. *"The grid on the ground has spotted it. They're sending up rocks to fight it."*

"They're rotten marksmen," said Calhoun. "They missed me!"

He aimed his ship. He knew the capacities of his ship as only a man who'd handled one for a long time could. He knew quite exactly what it could do.

The rocket from remoteness—the megaton-bomb guided missile—came smoking furiously from the stars. Calhoun seemed to throw his ship into a collision course. The rocket swerved to avoid him, though guided from many thousands of miles away. There was a trivial time-lag, too, between the time its scanners picked up a picture and transmitted it, and the transmission reached the Phaedrian fleet and the controlling impulses reached the missile in response. Calhoun counted on that. He had to. But he wasn't trying for a collision. He was forcing evasive action. He secured it. The rocket slanted itself to dart aside, and Calhoun threw the Med Ship into a flip-flop and—it was a hair-raising thing—slashed the rocket lengthwise with his rocket flame. That flame was less than half an inch thick, but it was of the temperature of the surface of a star, and in emptiness it was some hundreds of yards long. It sliced the rocket neatly. It flamed hideously, and even so far, Calhoun felt a cushioned impact from the flame. But that was the missile's rocket fuel. An atom bomb is the one known

69

kind of bomb which will not be exploded by being sliced in half.

The fragments of the guided missile went on toward the planet, but they were harmless.

"*All right!*" said the spacephone icily—but Calhoun thought there was relief in the voice. "*You've only delayed our landing and lost a good many lives to disease!*"

Calhoun swallowed something he suspected was his heart, come up into his throat.

"Now," he said, "we'll see if that's true!"

His ship had lost its spaceward velocity before it met the missile. Now it was gaining velocity toward the planet. He cut off the rocket to observe. He swung the hull about and gave a couple of short rocket blasts.

"I'd better get economical," he told Murgatroyd. "Rocket fuel is hard to come by, this far out in space. If I don't watch out, we'll be caught in orbit, here, with no way to get down! I don't think the local inhabitants would be inclined to help us."

His lateral dash at the missile had given him something close to orbital speed relative to the planet's surface, though. The Med Ship went floating, with seemingly infinite leisure, around the vast bulge of the embattled world. In less than half an hour it was deep in the blackness of Canis' nighttime shadow. In three-quarters of an hour it came out again at the sunrise edge, barely four hundred miles high.

"Not quite speed enough for a true orbit," he told Murgatroyd critically. "I'd give a lot for a good map!"

He watched alertly. He could gain more height if he needed to, but he was worried about rocket fuel. It is intended for dire emergencies only. It weighed too much to be carried in quantity.

He spotted the city of Canopolis on the horizon. He became furiously busy. He inverted the little ship and dived down into atmosphere. He killed speed with rocket flames and air friction together, falling recklessly the while. He was barely two miles high when he swept past a ridge of mountains and the city lay ahead and below. He could have crashed just short of it. But he spent more fuel to stay aloft. He used the rockets twice. Delicately.

At a ground speed of perhaps as little as two hundred miles an hour, supported at the end by a jetting, hair-thin rocket flame that was like a rod of electric arc-fire, he swept across the top of the landing grid. The swordlike flame washed briefly over the nearer edge. Very briefly. The flame cut a slash down through steel girders and heavy copper cables together. The rockets roared furiously. That one disabling cut at the grid had been on a downward, darting drift. Now the ship shouted, and swooped up, and on—and it swept above the far side of the grid only yards from the wide strip of copper which guided its force-fields out into space. Here it cut cables, girders, and force-field guide together for better than two hundred feet from the top. The grid was useless until painstaking labor had made the damage good.

Calhoun used nearly the last of his fuel for height while he said crisply on the spacephone:

"Calling fleet! Calling fleet! Med Ship calling fleet! I've disabled the landing grid on Canopolis! You can come in now and take care of the sick. There are no weapons aground to speak of and if you don't get trigger-happy there should be no fighting. I'll be landed off somewhere in the hills to the north of the town. If the local inhabitants don't pack explosives out and crack the ship to get at me, I'll have the facts on the antibody ready for you. In fact, as soon as I get down I'll give them to you by spacephone, just in case."

It was a near thing, though. His rocket fuel was exhausted when he hit the ground. The flame sputtered and stopped when the ship was three feet from touching. It fell over, splintering trees. It was distinctly a rough landing.

Murgatroyd was very indignant about it. He scolded

shrilly while Calhoun unstrapped himself from the chair and when he looked out to see where they were.

* * *

It was a week later when the Med Ship—brought to the grid for repair and refueling—was ready for space again. The original landing grid still stood, of course. But it was straddled and overwhelmed, huge as it was, by the utterly gigantic flying grid from Phaedra. There were not many ships aground, though. As Calhoun moved toward the control building, now connected by cable to the control quarters in the flying grid, one of the few ships remaining seemed to fall toward the sky. A second ship followed only seconds later.

He went into the control building. Walker the elder, from Phaedra, nodded remotely as he entered. The younger Walker scowled at him. He had been in consultation with his father, and the atmosphere was one of great reserve.

"Hm-m-m," said the elder Walker, gruffly. "What's the report?"

"Fairly good," said Calhoun. "There was one lot of antibody that seems to have been a trifle under strength. But the general situation seems satisfactory. There'll be a few more cases of one thing and another, of course—cases that are incubating now. But they'll do all right on the antibody shots. They have so far, at any rate." He said to the younger Walker, "You did a very good job rounding up the thirteen-to-fifteen-year-olds to escort the fleet doctors and handle the patients for them. They took themselves very seriously. They were ideal for the job. Your young-warrior group—"

"A lot of them," said young Walker dourly, "have taken to the woods. They swear they'll never give in!"

"How about the girls?"

Young Walker shrugged.

"They're fluttering about and beginning to talk about

72

clothes. When older women arrive there'll be dress-making—"

"And the lads in the woods," said Calhoun, "will come out to fascinate, and be fascinated instead. Do you think there'll be really much trouble?"

"No-o-o," said young Walker sourly. "Some of . . . our younger crowd seem relieved to be rid of responsibility."

"But," interposed the older Walker, gruffly, "he wants it. He thrives on it. He'll get it!" He hrrumphed. "The same with the others who showed what they could do here. We oldsters need them. We don't plan any . . . ah . . . reprisals."

Calhoun raised his eyebrows.

"Should I be surprised?"

The older Walker snorted.

"You didn't expect us to fall into each other's arms after what's happened, did you? No! But we are going to try to ignore our . . . differences as much as we can. We won't forget them, though."

"I suspect," said Calhoun, "that they'll be harder to remember than you think. You had a culture that split apart. Its pieces were incomplete—and a society has to be complete to survive. It isn't a human invention. It's something we have an instinct for—as birds have an instinct to build nests. When we build a culture according to our instincts, we get along. When that's impossible—there's trouble." Then he said, "I'm not trying to lecture you."

"Oh," said the elder Walker. "You aren't?"

Calhoun grinned.

"I thought I'd be the most unpopular man on this planet," he said cheerfully. "And I am. I interfered in everybody's business and nobody carried out his plans the way he wanted to. But at least nobody feels like he won. You'll be pleased when I lift the quarantine and take off, won't you?"

The older Walker said scornfully:

"We're paying no attention to your quarantine! Our

fleet's loading up our wives on Phaedra, to ferry them here as fast as overdrive will do it! D'you think we'd pay any attention to your quarantine?"

Calhoun grinned again. The younger Walker said painfully:

"I suppose you think we should—" He stopped, and said very carefully: "What you did was for our good, all right, but it hurts us more than it does you. In twenty years, maybe, we'll be able to laugh at ourselves. Then we'll feel grateful. Now we know what we owe you, but we don't like it."

"And that," said Calhoun, "means that everything is back to normal. That's the traditional attitude toward all medical men—owe them a lot and hate to pay. I'll sign the quarantine release and take off as soon as you give me some rocket fuel, just in case of emergency."

"Right away!" said the two Walkers, in unison.

Calhoun snapped his fingers. Murgatroyd swaggered to his side. Calhoun took the little *tormal's* black paw in his hand.

"Come along, Murgatroyd," he said cheerfully. "You're the only person I really treated badly, and you don't mind. I suppose the moral of all this is that a *tormal* is a man's best friend."

MED SHIP MAN

I.

Calhoun regarded the communicator with something like exasperation as his taped voice repeated a standard approach-call for the twentieth time. But no answer came, which had become irritating a long time ago. This was a new Med Service sector for Calhoun. He'd been assigned to another man's tour of duty because the other man had been taken down with romance. He'd gotten married, which ruled him out for Med Ship duty. So now Calhoun listened to his own voice endlessly repeating a call that should have been answered immediately.

Murgatroyd the *tormal* watched with beady, interested eyes. The planet Maya lay off to port of the Med Ship *Esclipus Twenty*. Its almost-circular disk showed full-size on a vision-screen beside the ship's controlboard. The image was absolutely clear and vividly colored. There was an ice-cap in view. There were continents. There were seas. The cloud-system of a considerable cyclonic disturbance could be noted off at one side, and the continents looked reasonably as they should, and the seas were of that muddy, indescribable tint which indicates deep water.

Calhoun's own voice, taped half an hour earlier, sounded in a speaker as it went again to the communicator and then to the extremely visible world a hundred thousand miles away.

"*Calling ground,*" said Calhoun's recorded voice. "*Med Ship* Esclipus Twenty *calling ground to report arrival*

75

and ask coördinates for landing. Our mass is fifty stand-
ard tons. Repeat, five-oh tons. Purpose of landing, plane-
tary health inspection."

The recorded voice stopped. There was silence except
for those also-taped random noises which kept the inside
of the ship from feeling like the inside of a tomb.

Murgatroyd said:

"Chee?"

Calhoun said ironically:

"Undoubtedly, Murgatroyd! Undoubtedly! Whoever's
on duty at the spaceport stepped out for a moment, or
dropped dead, or did something equally inconvenient.
We have to wait until he gets back or somebody else
takes over!"

Murgatroyd said *"Chee!"* again and began to lick his
whiskers. He knew that when Calhoun called on the
communicator, another human voice should reply. Then
there should be conversation, and shortly the force-
fields of a landing-grid should take hold of the Med Ship
and draw it planetward. In time it ought to touch ground
in a space-port with a gigantic, silvery landing-grid rising
skyward all about it. Then there should be people greet-
ing Calhoun cordially and welcoming Murgatroyd with
smiles and pettings.

"Calling ground," said the recorded voice yet again.
"Med Ship Esclipus Twenty—."

It went on through the formal notice of arrival. Murgatroyd waited in pleasurable anticipation. When the Med
Ship arrived at a port of call humans gave him sweets
and cakes, and they thought it charming that he drank
coffee just like a human, only with more gusto. Aground,
Murgatroyd moved zestfully in society while Calhoun
worked. Calhoun's work was conferences with planetary
health officials, politely receiving such information as
they thought important, and tactfully telling them about
the most recent developments in medical science as
known to the Interstellar Medical Service.

"Somebody," said Calhoun darkly, "is going to catch the devil for this!"

The communicator loud-speaker spoke abruptly.

"*Calling Med Ship*," said a voice. "*Calling Med Ship Esclipus Twenty! Liner Candida calling. Have you had an answer from ground?*"

Calhoun blinked. Then he said curtly:

"Not yet. I've been callling all of half an hour, too!"

"*We've been in orbit twelve hours,*" said the voice from emptiness. "*Calling all the while. No answer. We don't like it.*"

Calhoun flipped a switch that threw a vision-screen into circuit with the ship's electron telescope. A star-field appeared and shifted wildly. Then a bright dot centered itself. He raised the magnification. The bright dot swelled and became a chubby commercial ship, with the false ports that passengers like to believe they look through when in space. Two relatively large cargo-ports on each side showed that it carried heavy freight in addition to passengers. It was one of those work-horse intra-cluster ships that distribute the freight and passengers the long-haul liners dump off only at established transshipping ports.

Murgatroyd padded across the Med Ship's cabin and examined the image with a fine air of wisdom. It did not mean anything to him, but he said, "*Chee!*" as if making an observation of profound significance. He went back to the cushion on which he'd been curled up.

"*We don't see anything wrong aground,*" the liner's voice complained, "*but they don't answer calls! We don't get any scatter-signals either! We went down to two diameters and couldn't pick up a thing! And we have a passenger to land! He insists on it!*"

By ordinary, communications between different places on a planet's surface use frequencies the ion-layers of the atmosphere either reflect or refract down past the horizon. But there is usually some small leakage to space, and line-of-sight frequencies are generally abundant. It is one of the annoyances of a ship coming in to port that space near most planets is usually full of local signals.

"I'll check," said Calhoun curtly. "Stand by."

The *Candida* would have arrived off Maya as the Med Ship had done, and called down as Calhoun had been doing. It was very probably a ship on schedule and the grid operator at the space-port should have expected it. Space-commerce was important to any planet, comparing more or less with the export-import business of an industrial nation in ancient times on Earth. Planets had elaborate traffic-aid systems for the cargo-carriers which moved between solar systems as they'd once moved between continents on Earth. Such traffic aids were very carefully maintained. Certainly for a space-port landing-grid not to respond to calls for twelve hours running seemed ominous.

"*We've been wondering,*" said the *Candida* querilously, "*if there could be something radically wrong below. Sickness, for example.*"

The word "sickness" was a substitute for a more alarming word. But a plague had nearly wiped out the population of Dorset, once upon a time, and the first ships to arrive after it had broken out most incautiously went down to ground, and so carried the plague to their next two ports of call. Nowadays quarantine regulations were enforced very strictly indeed.

"I'll try to find out what's the matter," said Calhoun.

"*We've got a passenger,*" repeated the *Candida* aggrievedly, "*who insists that we land him by space-boat if we don't make a ship-landing. He says he has important business aground.*"

Calhoun did not answer. The rights of passengers were extravagantly protected, these days. To fail to deliver a passenger to his destination entitled him to punitive damages which no space-line could afford. So the Med Ship would seem heaven-sent to the *Candida*'s skipper. Calhoun could relieve him of responsibility.

78

The telescope screen winked, and showed the surface of the planet a hundred thousand miles away. Calhoun glanced at the image on the port screen and guided the telescope to the space-port city—Maya City. He saw highways and blocks of buildings. He saw the space-port and its landing-grid. He could see no motion, of course. He raised the magnification. He raised it again. Still no motion. He upped the magnification until the lattice-pattern of the telescope's amplifying crystal began to show. But at the ship's distance from the planet, a ground-car would represent only the fortieth of a second of arc. There was atmosphere, too, with thermals. Anything the size of a ground-car simply couldn't be seen.

But the city showed quite clearly. Nothing massive had happened to it. No large-scale physical disaster had occurred. It simply did not answer calls from space.

Calhoun flipped off the screen.

"I think," he said irritably into the communicator microphone, "I suspect I'll have to make an emergency-landing. It could be something as trivial as a power failure."—But he knew that was wildly improbable.—"Or it could be—anything. I'll land on rockets and tell you what I find."

The voice from the *Candida* said hopefully:

"Can you authorize us to refuse to land our passenger for his own protection? He's raising the devil! He insists that his business demands that he be landed."

A word from Calhoun as a Med Service man would protect the space-liner from a claim for damages. But Calhoun didn't like the look of things. He realized, distastefully, that he might find practically anything down below. He might find that he had to quarantine the planet and himself with it. In such a case he'd need the *Candida* to carry word of the quarantine to other planets and get word to Med Service sector headquarters.

"We've lost a lot of time," insisted the *Candida*. *"Can you authorize us—"*

79

"Not yet," said Calhoun. "I'll tell you when I land."

"*But—*"

"I'm signing off for the moment," said Calhoun. "Stand by."

He headed the little ship downward and as it gathered velocity he went over the briefing-sheets covering this particular world. He'd never touched ground here before. His occupation, of course, was seeing to the dissemination of medical science as it developed under the Med Service. The Service itself was neither political nor administrative, but it was important. Every human-occupied world was supposed to have a Med Ship visit at least once in four years. Such visits verified the state of public health. Med Ship men like Calhoun offered advice on public-health problems. When something out of the ordinary turned up, the Med Service had a staff of researchers who hadn't been wholly baffled yet. There were great ships which could carry the ultimate in laboratory equipment and specialized personnel to any place where they were needed. Not less than a dozen inhabited worlds in this sector alone owed the survival of their populations to the Med Service, and the number of those which couldn't have been colonized without Med Service help was legion.

Calhoun re-read the briefing. Maya was one of four planets in this general area whose life-systems seemed to have had a common origin, suggesting that the Arrhenius theory of space-traveling spores was true in some limited sense. A genus of ground-cover plants with motile stems and leaves, and cannibalistic tendencies, was considered strong evidence of common origin.

The planet had been colonized for two centuries, now, and produced organic compounds of great value from indigenous plants. They were used in textile manufacture. There were no local endemic infections to which men were susceptive. A number of human-use crops were grown. Cereals, grasses and grains, however, could not be grown because of the native ground-cover motile-stem plants. All wheat and cereal food had to be imported, and the fact severely limited Maya's population. There were about two million on the planet, settled on a peninsular in the Yucatan Sea and a small area of mainland. Public-health surveys had shown such-and-such, and such-and-such, and thus-and-so. There was no mention of anything to account for the failure of the spaceport to respond to arrival-calls from space. Naturally!

The Med Ship drove on down. The planet revolved beneath it. As Maya's sunlit hemisphere enlarged, Calhoun kept the telescope's field wide. He saw cities and vast areas of cleared land where native plants were grown as raw materials for the organics' manufacturies. He saw very little true chlorophyl green, though. Mayan foliage tended to a dark, olive-green.

At fifty miles he was sure that the city streets were empty even of ground-car traffic. There was no spaceship aground in the landing-grid. There were no ground-cars in motion on the splendid, multiple-lane highways.

At thirty miles altitude there were still no signals in the atmosphere, though when he tried amplitude-modulation reception he picked up static. But there was no normally modulated signal on the air at any frequency. At twenty miles, no. At fifteen miles broadcast power was available, which proved that the landing-grid was working as usual, tapping the upper atmosphere for electric charges to furnish power for all the planet's needs.

From ten miles down to ground-touch, Calhoun was busy. It is not too difficult to land a ship on rockets, with reasonably level ground to land on. But landing at a specific spot is something else. Calhoun juggled the ship to descend inside the grid aground. His rockets burned out pencil-thin holes through the clay and stone beneath the tarmac. He cut them off.

Silence. Stillness. The Med Ship's outside microphones picked up small noises of wind blowing over the city. There was no other sound at all.

—No. There was a singularly deliberate clicking sound, not loud and not fast. Perhaps a click—a double-click—every two seconds. That was all.

Calhoun went into the airlock with Murgatroyd frisking a little in the expectation of great social success among the people of this world. Calhoun cracked the outer airlock door. He smelled something. It was a faintly sour, astringent odor that had the quality of decay in it. But it was no kind of decay he recognized. Again stillness and silence. No traffic-noise. Not even the almost inaudible murmur that every city has in all its ways at all hours. The buildings looked as buildings should look at daybreak, except that the doors and windows were open. It was somehow shocking.

A ruined city is dramatic. An abandoned city is pathetic. This was neither. It was something new. It felt as if everybody had walked away, out of sight, within the past few minutes.

Calhoun headed for the space-port building with Murgatroyd ambling puzzledly at his side. Murgatroyd was disturbed. There should be people here! They should welcome Calhoun and admire him—Murgatroyd—and he should be a social lion with all the sweets he could eat and all the coffee he could put into his expandable belly. But nothing happened. Nothing at all.

"Chee?" he asked anxiously. "Chee-chee?"

"They've gone away," growled Calhoun. "They probably left in ground-cars. There's not a one in sight."

There wasn't. Calhoun could look out through the grid foundations and see long, sunlit, and absolutely empty streets. He arrived at the space-port building. There was —there had been—a green space about the base of the structure. There was not a living plant left. Leaves were wilted and limp. There was almost a jelly of collapsed stems and blossoms, of dark olive-green. The plants were dead, but not long enough to have dried up. They might have wilted two days before. Possibly three.

Calhoun went in the building. The space-port log lay open on a desk. It recorded the arrival of freight to be shipped away—undoubtedly—on the *Candida* now uneasily in orbit somewhere aloft. There was no sign of disorder. It was exactly as if the people here had walked out to look at something interesting, and hadn't come back.

Calhoun trudged out of the space-port and to the streets and buildings of the city proper. It was incredible! Doors were opened or unlocked. Merchandise in the shops lay on display, exactly as it had been spread out to interest customers. There was no sign of confusion anywhere. Even in a restaurant there were dishes and flatware on the tables. The food in the plates was stale, as if three days old, but it hadn't yet begun to spoil. The appearance of everything was as if people at their meals had simply, at some signal, gotten up and walked out without any panic or disturbance.

Calhoun made a wry face. He'd remembered something. Among the tales that had been carried from Earth to the other worlds of the galaxy there was a completely unimportant mystery-story which people still sometimes tried to write an ending to. It was the story of an ancient sailing-ship called the *Marie Celeste*, which was found sailing aimlessly in the middle of the ocean. There was food on the cabin table and the galley stove was still warm, and there was no sign of any trouble, or terror, or disturbance which might cause the ship to be abandoned. But there was not a living soul on board. Nobody had ever been able to contrive a believable explanation.

"Only," said Calhoun to Murgatroyd, "this is on a larger scale. The people of this city walked out about three days ago, and didn't come back. Maybe all the people on the planet did the same, since there's not a communicator in operation anywhere. To make the understatement of the century, Murgatroyd, I don't like this! I don't like it a bit!"

On the way back to the Med Ship, Calhoun stopped at another place where, on a grass-growing planet, there would have been green sward. There were Earth-type trees, and some native ones, and between them there should have been a lawn. The trees were thriving, but the ground-cover plants were collapsed and rotting. Calhoun picked up a bit of the semi-slime and smelled it. It had a faintly sour and astringent smell, the same he'd noticed when he opened the airlock door. He threw the stuff away and brushed off his hands. Something had killed the ground-cover plants which had the habit of killing Earth-type grass when planted here.

He listened. Everywhere that humans live, there are insects and birds and other tiny creatures which are essential parts of the ecological system to which the human race is adjusted. They have to be carried to and established upon every new world that mankind hopes to occupy. But there was no sound of such living creatures here. It was probable that the bellowing roar of the Med Ship's emergency rockets was the only real noise the city had heard since its people went away.

The stillness bothered Murgatroyd. He said, *"Chee!"* in a subdued tone and stayed close to Calhoun. Calhoun shook his head. Then he said abruptly;

"Come along, Murgatroyd!"

He went back to the grid and the building housing its controls. He didn't look at the space-port log this time. He went to the instruments recording the second function of a landing-grid. In addition to lifting up and letting down ships of space, a landing-grid drew down power from the ions of the upper atmosphere, and broadcast it. It provided all the energy that humans on a world could need. It was solar power, in a way, absorbed and stored by a layer of ions miles high, which then could be drawn on and distributed by the grid. During his descent Calhoun had noted that broadcast power was still available. Now he looked at what the instruments said.

The needle on the dial showing power-drain moved slowly back and forth. It was a rythmic movement, going from maximum to minimum power-use, and then back again. Approximately six million kilowatts was being taken out of the broadcast every two seconds for the half of one second. Then the drain cut off for a second and a half, and went on again—for half a second.

Frowning, Calhoun raised his eyes to a very fine color photograph on the wall above the power dials. It was a picture of the human-occupied part of Maya, taken four thousand miles out in space. It had been enlarged to four feet by six, and Maya City could be seen as an irregular group of squares and triangles measuring a little more than half an inch by three-quarters. The detail was perfect. It was possible to see perfectly straight, infinitely thin lines moving out from the city. They were multiple-lane highways, mathematically straight from one city to another, and then mathematically straight—even though at a new angle—until the next. Calhoun stared thoughtfully at them.

"The people left the city in a hurry," he told Murgatroyd, "and there was little confusion, if any. So they knew in advance that they might have to go, and were ready for it. If they took anything, they had it ready-packed in their cars. But they hadn't been sure they'd have to go because they were going about their businesses as usual. All the shops were open and people were eating in restaurants, and so on."

Murgatroyd said, "*Chee!*" as if in full agreement.

"Now," demanded Calhoun, "where did they go? The question's really that of where they could go! There were about eight hundred thousand people in this city. There'd be cars for everyone, of course, and two hundred thousand cars would take everybody. But that's a lot of ground-cars! Put 'em two hundred feet apart on a highway, and that's twenty-six cars to the mile on each lane.

. . . Run them at a hundred miles an hour on a twelve-lane road—using all lanes one way—and that's twenty-six hundred cars per lane per hour, and that's thirty-one thousand . . . Two highways make sixty-two . . . Three highways . . . With two highways they could empty the city in under three hours, and with three highways close to two . . . Since there's no sign of panic, that's what they must have done. Must have worked it out in advance, too. Maybe they'd done it before. . . ."

He searched the photograph which was so much more detailed than a map. There were mountains to the north of Maya City, but only one highway led north. There were more mountains to the west. One highway went into them, but not through. To the south there was sea, which curved around some three hundred miles from Maya City and made the human colony on Maya into a peninsular. It was a small fraction of the planet, but grains wouldn't grow there. The planet could grow native plants for raw material for organic chemicals, but it couldn't grow all its own food so its population was limited.

"They went east," said Calhoun presently. He traced lines with his finger. "Three highways go east. There's the only way they could go, quickly. They hadn't been sure they'd have to go but they knew where to go when they did. So when they got their warning, they left. On three highways, to the east. And we'll follow them and ask what the hell they ran away from. Nothing's visible here!"

He went back to the Med Ship, Murgatroyd skipping with him. As the airlock door closed behind them, he heard a click from the outside-microphone speakers. He listened. It was a doubled clicking, as of something turned on and almost at once turned off again. There was a two-second cycle—the same as that of the power-drain. Something drawing six million kilowatts went on and immediately off again every two seconds. It made a sound in speakers linked to outside microphones, but it didn't make a noise in the air. The microphone clicks were induction; pick-up; like cross-talk on defective telephone cables.

.Calhoun shrugged his shoulders almost up to his ears. He went to the communicator.

"Calling *Candida*—" he began, and the answer almost leaped down his throat.

"*Candida to Med Ship. Come in! Come in! What's happened down there?*"

"The city's deserted without any sign of panic," said Calhoun, "and there's power and nothing seems to be broken down. But it's as if somebody had said, 'Everybody clear out' and they did. That doesn't happen on a whim! What's your next port of call?"

The *Candida's* voice told him, hopefully.

"Take a report," commanded Calhoun. "Deliver it to the public-health office immediately you land. They'll get it to Med Service sector headquarters. I'm going to stay here and find out what's been going on."

He dictated, growing irritated as he did so because he couldn't explain what he reported. Something serious had taken place, but there was no clue as to what it was. Strictly speaking, it wasn't certainly a public-health affair. But any emergency the size of this one involved public-health factors.

"I'm remaining aground to investigate," finished Calhoun. "I will report further when or if it is possible. Message ends."

"*What about our passenger?*"

"To the devil with your passenger!" said Calhoun peevishly. "Do as you please!"

He cut off the communicator and prepared for activity outside the ship. Presently he and Murgatroyd went to look for transportation. The Med Ship couldn't be used for a search operation. It didn't carry enough rocket-fuel. They'd have to use a ground vehicle.

It was again shocking to note that nothing had moved but sun-shadows. Again it seemed that everybody had simply walked out of some door or other and failed to come back. Calhoun saw the windows of jewellers' shops. Treasures lay unguarded in plain view. He saw a florist's shop. Here there were earth-type flowers apparently thriving, and some strangely beautiful flowers with olive-green foliage which throve as well as the Earth-plants. There was a cage in which a plant had grown, and that plant was wilting and about to rot. But a plant that had to be grown in a cage. . . .

He found a ground-car agency, perhaps for imported cars, perhaps for those built on Maya. He went in. There were cars on display. He chose one,—an elaborate sports car. He turned its key and it hummed. He drove it carefully out into the empty street. Murgatroyd sat interestedly beside him.

"This is luxury, Murgatroyd," said Calhoun. "Also it's grand theft. We medical characters can't usually afford such things or have an excuse to steal them. But these are parlous times. We take a chance."

"*Chee!*" said Murgatroyd.

"We want to find a fugitive population and ask what they ran away from. As of the moment, it seems that they ran away from nothing. They may be pleased to know they can come back."

Murgatroyd again said, "*Chee!*"

Calhoun drove through vacant ways. It was somehow nerve-racking. He felt as if someone should pop out and say, "Boo!" at any instant. He discovered an elevated highway and a ramp leading up to it. It ran west to east. He drove eastward, watching sharply for any sign of life. There was none.

He was nearly out of the city when he felt the chest-impact of a sonic boom, and then heard a trailing-away growling sound which seemed to come from farther away as it died out. It was the result of something travelling faster than sound, so that the noise it made far away had to catch up with the sound it emitted nearby.

He stared up. He saw a parachute blossom as a bare

88

speck against the blue. Then he heard the even deeper-toned roaring of a supersonic craft climbing skyward. It could be a spaceliner's lifeboat, descended into atmosphere and going out again. It was. It had left a parachute behind and now went back to space to rendezvous with its parent ship.

"That," said Calhoun impatiently, "will be the *Candida's* passenger. If he was insistent enough—."

He scowled. The *Candida's* voice had said its passenger demanded to be landed for business reasons. And Calhoun had a prejudice against some kinds of business men who would think their own affairs more important than anything else. Two standard years before, he'd made a planetary health inspection on Texia II, in another galactic sector. It was a llano planet and a single giant business enterprise. Illimitable prairies had been sown with an Earth-type grass which destroyed the native ground-cover—the reverse of the ground-cover situation here—and the entire planet was a monstrous range for beef-cattle. Dotted about were gigantic slaughter-houses, and cattle in masses of tens of thousands were shifted here and there by ground-induction fields which acted as fences. Ultimately the cattle were driven by these same induction-fences to the slaughter-houses and actually into the chutes where their throats were slit. Every imaginable fraction of a credit profit was extracted from their carcasses, and Calhoun had found it appalling. He was not sentimental about cattle, but the complete cold-bloodedness of the entire operation sickened him. The same cold-bloodedness was practiced toward the human employees who ran the place. Their living-quarters were sub-marginal. The air stank of cattle-murder. Men worked for the Texia Company or they did not work. If they did not work they did not eat. If they worked and ate,—Calhoun could see nothing satisfying in being alive on a world like that! His report to Med Service had been biting. He'd been prejudiced against business men ever since.

89

But a parachute descended, blowing away from the city. It would land not too far from the highway he followed. And it didn't occur to Calhoun not to help the unknown chutist. He saw a small figure dangling below the chute. He slowed the ground-car. He estimated where the parachute would land.

He was off the twelve-lane highway and on a feeder-road when the chute was a hundred feet high. He was racing across a field of olive-green plants—the field went all the way to the horizon—when the parachute actually touched ground. There was a considerable wind. The man in the harness bounced. He didn't know how to spill the air. The chute dragged him.

Calhoun sped ahead, swerved, and ran into the chute. He stopped the car and the chute stopped with it. He got out.

The man lay in a helpless tangle of cordage. He thrust unskilfully at it. When Calhoun came up he said suspiciously:

"Have you a knife?"

Calhoun offered a knife, politely opening its blade. The man slashed at the cords. He freed himself. There was an attache-case lashed to his chute-harness. He cut at those cords. The attache-case not only came clear, but opened. It dumped out an incredible mass of brand-new, tightly-packed interstellar credit certificates. Calhoun could see that the denominations were one-thousand and ten-thousand credits. The man from the chute reached under his armpit and drew out a blaster. It was not a service weapon. It was elaborate. It was practically a toy. With a dour glance at Calhoun he put it in a side pocket and gathered up the scattered money. It was an enormous sum, but he packed it back. He stood up.

"My name is Allison," he said in an authoritative voice. "Arthur Allison. I'm much obliged. Now I'll get you to take me to Maya City."

"No," said Calhoun politely. "I just left there. It's deserted. I'm not going back. There's nobody there."

"But I've important bus—." The other man stared. "It's deserted? But that's impossible!"

"Quite," agreed Calhoun, "but it's true. It's abandoned. It's uninhabited. Everybody's left it. There's none there at all."

The man who called himself Allison blinked unbelievingly. He swore. Then he raged profanely. But he was not bewildered by the news. Which, upon consideration, was itself almost bewildering. But then his eyes grew shrewd. He looked about him.

"My name is Allison," he repeated, as if there were some sort of magic in the word. "Arthur Allison. No matter what's happened, I've some business to do here. Where have the people gone? I need to find—."

"I need to find them too," said Calhoun. "I'll take you with me, if you like."

"You've heard of me." It was a statement, confidently made.

"Never," said Calhoun politely. "If you're not hurt, suppose you get in the car? I'm as anxious as you are to find out what's happened. I'm Med Service."

Allison moved toward the car.

"Med Service, eh? I don't think much of the Med Service! You people try to meddle in things that are none of your business!"

Calhoun did not answer. The muddy man, clutching the attache-case tightly, waded through the olive-green plants to the car and climbed in. Murgatroyd said cordially: "*Chee-chee!*" but Allison viewed him with distaste.

"What's this?"

"He's Murgatroyd," said Calhoun. "He's a *tormal*. He's Med Service personnel."

"I don't like beasts," said Allison coldly.

"He's much more important to me than you are," said Calhoun, "if the matter should come to a test."

Allison stared at him as if expecting him to cringe. Calhoun did not. Allison showed every sign of being an important man who expected his importance to be recognized and catered to. When Calhoun stirred impatiently he got into the car and growled a little. Calhoun took his place. The ground-car hummed. It rose on the six columns of air which took the place of wheels. It went across the field of dark-green plants, leaving the parachute deflated across a number of rows, and a trail of crushed-down plants where it had moved.

It reached the highway again. Calhoun ran the car up on the highway's shoulder, and then suddenly checked. He'd noticed something. He stopped the car and got out. Where the ploughed field ended, and before the coated surface of the highway began, there was a space where on another world one would expect to see green grass. On this planet grass did not grow. But there would normally be some sort of self-planted vegetation where there was soil and sunshine and moisture. There had been such vegetation here, but now there was only a thin, repellant mass of slimy and decaying foliage. Calhoun bent down to it. It had a sour, faintly astringent smell of decay. These were the ground-cover plants of Maya of which Calhoun had read. They had motile stems and leaves and flowers. They had cannibalistic tendencies. They were dead. But they were the local weeds which made it impossible to grow grain for human use upon this world.

Calhoun straightened up and returned to the car. Plants like this were wilted at the base of the spaceport building, and on another place where there should have been sward. Calhoun had seen a large dead member of the genus in a florist's. It had been growing in a cage before it died. There was a singular coincidence, here. Humans ran away from something, and something caused the death of a particular genus of cannibal weeds.

It did not exactly add up to anything in particular, and certainly wasn't evidence for anything at all. But Calhoun drove on in a vaguely puzzled mood. The germ of a guess was forming in his mind. He couldn't pretend to himself that it was likely, but it was surely no more unlikely than most of two million human beings abandoning their homes at a moment's notice.

3.

They came to the turn-off for a town called Tenochitlan, some forty miles from Maya City. Calhoun swung off the highway to go through it. Whoever had chosen the name Maya for this planet had been interested in the legends of Yucatan, back on Earth. There were many instances of such hobbies in a Med Ship's list of ports of call. Calhoun touched ground regularly on planets named for counties and towns when men first roamed the stars and nostalgically christened their discoveries with names suggested by homesickness. There was a Tralee, and a Dorset, and an Eire. Colonists not infrequently took their world's given name as a pattern and chose related names for seas and peninsulars and mountain-chains. Calhoun had even visited a world called Texia where the landing-grid rose near a town called Corral and the principal meat-packing settlement was named Roundup.

Whatever the name Tenochitlan would have suggested, though, was denied by the town itself. It was a small town. It had a pleasing local type of architecture. There were shops and some factories, and many strictly private homes, some clustered close together and others in the middles of considerable gardens. In those gardens also there was wilt and decay among the cannibal plants. There was no grass, because such plants prevented it, but now the plants preventing grasses themselves were dead. Except for the one class of killed growing things, however, vegetation was luxuriant.

But the little city was deserted. Its streets were empty. Its houses were untenanted. Some houses were apparently locked up, here, though, and Calhoun saw three or four shops whose stock-in-trade had been covered over before the owners departed. He guessed that either this town had been warned earlier than the space-port city, or else they knew they had time to get in motion before the highways were filled with the cars from the west.

Allison looked at the houses with keen, evaluating eyes. He did not seem to notice the absence of people. When Calhoun swung back on the great road beyond the little city, Allison regarded the endless fields of dark-green plants with much the same sort of interest.

"Interesting," he said abruptly when Tenochitlan fell behind and dwindled to a speck. "Very interesting. I'm interested in land. Real property. That's my business. I've a land-owning corporation on Thanet Three. I've some holdings on Dorset, too. And elsewhere. It just occurred to me. What's all this land and the cities worth with the people all run away?"

"What," asked Calhoun, "are the people worth who've run?"

Allison paid no attention. He looked shrewd. Thoughtful.

"I came here to buy land," he said. "I'd arranged to buy some hundreds of square miles. I'd buy more if the price were right. But—as things are, it looks like the price of land ought to go down quite a bit. Quite a bit!"

"It depends," said Calhoun, "on whether there's anybody left alive to sell it to you, and what sort of thing has happened."

Allison looked at him sharply.

"Ridiculous!" he said authoritatively. "There's no question of their being alive!"

"They thought there might be," observed Calhoun. "That's why they ran away. They hoped they'd be safe where they ran to. I hope they are."

Allison ignored the comment. His eyes remained intent and shrewd. He was not bewildered by the flight of the people of Maya. His mind was busy with contemplation of that flight from the standpoint of a man of business.

The car went racing onward. The endless fields of dark green rushed past to the rear. The highway was deserted. There were three strips of surfaced road, mathematically straight, going on to the horizon. They went on by tens and scores of miles. Each strip was wide enough to allow four ground-cars to run side by side. The highway was intended to allow all the produce of all these fields to be taken to market or a processing plant at the highest possible speed and in any imaginable quantity. The same roads had allowed the cities to be deserted instantly the warning—whatever the warning was—arrived.

Fifty miles beyond Tenochitlan there was a mile-long strip of sheds. They contained agricultural machinery for crop-culture and trucks to carry the crops to where they belonged. There was no sign of life about the machinery. There was no sign of life in a further hour's run to westward.

Then there was a city visible to the left. But it was not served by this particular highway, but another. There was no sign of any movement in its streets. It moved along the horizon to the left and rear. Presently it disappeared.

Half an hour later still, Murgatroyd said:

"*Chee!*"

He stirred uneasily. A moment later he said, "*Chee!*" again.

Calhoun turned his eyes from the road. Murgatroyd looked unhappy. Calhoun ran his hand over the *tormal's* furry body. Murgatroyd pressed against him. The car raced on. Murgatroyd whimpered a little. Calhoun's fingers felt the little animal's muscles tense sharply, and then relax, and after a little tense again. Murgatroyd said almost hysterically:

"*Chee-chee-chee-chee!*"

Calhoun stopped the car, but Murgatroyd did not seem to be relieved. Allison said impatiently:

"What's the matter?"

"That's what I'm trying to find out," said Calhoun. He felt Murgatroyd's pulse, and timed it with his sweep-second watch. He timed the muscular spasms that Murgatroyd displayed. They coincided with disturbances in his heart-beat. They came at approximately two-sec-cond intervals, and the tautening of the muscles lasted just about half a second.

"But I don't feel it!" said Calhoun.

Murgatroyd whimpered again and said, "*Chee-chee!*"

"What's going on?" demanded Allison, with the im-patience of a very important man indeed. "If the beast's sick, he's sick! I've got to find—."

Calhoun opened his med kit and went carefully through it. He found what he needed. He put a pill into Murgatroyd's mouth.

"Swallow it!" he commanded.

Murgatroyd resisted, but the pill went down. Calhoun watched him sharply. Murgatroyd's digestive system was delicate, but it was dependable. Anything that might be poisonous, Murgatroyd's stomach rejected instantly. But the pill stayed down.

"Look!" said Allison indignantly. "I've got business to do! In this attache-case I have some millions of inter-stellar credits, in cash, to pay down on purchases of land and factories! I ought to make some damned good deals! And I figure that that's as important as anything else you can think of! It's a damned sight more important than a beast with a belly-ache!"

Calhoun looked at him coldly.

"Do you own land on Texia?" he asked.

Allison's mouth dropped open. Extreme suspicion and unease appeared on his face. As a sign of the unease, his hand went to the side coat pocket in which he'd put a blaster. He didn't pluck it out. Calhoun's left fist swung around and landed. He took Allison's elaborate pocket-blaster and threw it away among the monotonous rows of olive-green plants. He returned to absorbed observa-tion of Murgatroyd.

In five minutes the muscular spasms diminished. In ten, Murgatroyd frisked. But he seemed to think that Calhoun had done something remarkable. In the warmest of tones he said:

"*Chee!*"

"Very good," said Calhoun. "We'll go ahead. I suspect you'll do as well as we do,—for a while."

The car lifted the few inches the air-columns sustained it above the ground. It went on, still to the eastward. But Calhoun drove more slowly, now.

"Something was giving Murgatroyd rythmic muscular spasms," he said coldly. "I gave him medication to stop them. He's more sensitive than we are so he reacted to a stimulus we haven't noticed yet. But I think we'll notice it presently."

Allison seemed to be dazed at the affront given him. It appeared to be unthinkable that anybody might lay hands on him.

"What the devil has that to do with me?" he demanded angrily. "And what did you hit me for? You're going to pay for this!"

"Until I do," Calhoun told him, "you'll be quiet. And it does have the devil to do with you. There was a Med Service gadget, once,—a tricky little device to produce contraction of chosen muscles. It was useful for re-starting stopped hearts without the need of an operation. It regulated the beat of hearts that were too slow or dangerously irregular. But some business man had a bright idea and got a tame researcher to link that gadget to ground induction currents. I suspect you know that business man!"

"I don't know what you're talking about," snapped Allison. But he was singularly tense.

"I do," said Calhoun unpleasantly. "I made a public-health inspection on Texia a couple of years ago. The whole planet is a single, gigantic, cattle-raising enterprise. They don't use metal fences. The herds are too big to be stopped by such things. They don't use cowboys. They cost money. On Texia they use ground-induction and the Med Service gadget linked together to serve

97

as cattle fences. They act like fences, though they're projected through the ground. Cattle become uncomfortable when they try to cross them. So they draw back. So men control them. They move them from place to place by changing the cattle-fences which are currents induced in the ground. The cattle have to keep moving or be punished by the moving fence. They're even driven into the slaughterhouse chutes by ground-induction fields! That's the trick on Texia, where induction fields herd cattle. I think it's the trick on Maya, where people are herded like cattle and driven out of their cities so the value of their fields and factories will drop,—so a land-buyer can find bargains!"

"You're insane!" snapped Allison. "I just landed on this planet! You saw me land! I don't know what happened before I got here! How could I?"

"You might have arranged it," said Calhoun.

Allison assumed an air of offended and superior dignity. Calhoun drove the car onward at very much less than the headlong pace he'd been keeping to. Presently he looked down at his hands on the steering-wheel. Now and then the tendons to his fingers seemed to twitch. At rythmic intervals, the skin crawled on the back of his hands. He glanced at Allison. Allison's hands were tightly clenched.

"There's a ground-induction fence in action, all right," said Calhoun calmly. "You notice? It's a cattle-fence and we're running into it. If we were cattle, now, we'd turn around and move away."

"I don't know what you're talking about!" said Allison.

But his hands stayed clenched. Calhoun slowed the car still more. He began to feel, all over his body, that every muscle tended to twitch at the same time. It was a horrible sensation. His heart-muscles tended to contract too, simultaneously with the rest, but one's heart has its own beat-rate. Sometimes the normal beat coincided with the twitch. Then his heart pounded violently,—so violently that it was painful. But equally often the imposed contraction of the heart-muscles came just after a normal contraction, and then it stayed tightly knotted for half a second. It missed a beat, and the feeling was agony. No animal would have pressed forward in the face of such sensations. It would have turned back long ago.

Calhoun stopped the car. He looked at Murgatroyd. Murgatroyd was completely himself. He looked inquiringly at Calhoun. Calhoun nodded to him, but he spoke—with some difficulty—to Allison.

"We'll see—if this thing—builds up.—You know that it's the Texia—trick. A ground—induction unit set up—here. It drove people—like cattle. Now we've—run into it.—It's holding people—like cattle."

He panted. His chest-muscles contracted with the rest, so that his breathing was interfered with. But Murgatroyd, who'd been made uneasy and uncomfortable before Calhoun noticed anything wrong, was now bright and frisky. Medication had desensitized his muscles to outside stimuli. He would be able to take a considerable electric shock without responding to it. But he could be killed by one that was strong enough.

A savage anger filled Calhoun. Everything fitted together. Allison had put his hand convenient to his blaster when Calhoun mentioned Texia. It meant that Calhoun suspected what Allison knew to be true. A cattle-fence unit had been set up on Maya, and it was holding—like cattle—the people it had previously driven like cattle. Calhoun could even deduce with some precision exactly what had been done. The first experience of Maya with the cattle-fence would have been with a very mild version of it. It would have been low-power and cause just enough uneasiness to be noticed. It would have been moved from west to east, slowly, and it would have reached a certain spot and there faded out. And it would have been a mystery and an uncomfortable thing, and nobody would understand it on Maya. In a week it would almost be forgotten. But then there'd come a stronger disturbance. And it would travel like the first one; down the length of the peninsular on which the colony lay, but stopping at the same spot as before, and then fading away to nothingness. And this also would have seemed mysterious but nobody would suspect humans of causing it. There'd be theorizing and much questioning, but it would be considered an unfamiliar natural event.

Probably the third use of the cattle-fence would be most disturbing. This time it would be acutely painful. But it would move into the cities and through them and past them,—and it would go down the peninsular to where it had stopped and faded on two previous occasions. And the people of Maya would be disturbed and scared. But they considered that they knew it began to the westward of Maya City, and moved toward the east at such-and-such a speed, and it went so far and no farther. And they would organize themselves to apply this carefully-worked-out information. And it would not occur to any of them that they had learned how to be driven like cattle.

Calhoun, of course, could only reason that this must have happened. But nothing else could have taken place. Perhaps there were more than three uses of the moving cattle-fence to get the people prepared to move past the known place at which it always faded to nothingness. They might have been days apart, or weeks apart, or months. There might have been stronger manifestations followed by weaker ones and then stronger ones again. But there was a cattle-fence—an inductive cattle-fence—across the highway here. Calhoun had driven into it. Every two seconds the muscles of his body tensed. Sometimes his heart missed a beat at the time that his breathing stopped, and sometimes it pounded violently. It seemed that the symptoms became more and more unbearable.

He got out his med kit, with hands that spasmodically jerked uncontrollably. He fumbled out the same medication he'd given Murgatroyd. He took two of the pellets.

"In reason," he said coldly, "I ought to let you take what this damned thing would give you. But—here!"

Allison had panicked. The idea of a cattle-fence suggested discomfort, of course. But it did not imply danger. The experience of a cattle-fence, designed for huge hoofed beasts instead of men, was terrifying. Allison gasped. He made convulsive movements. Calhoun himself moved erratically. For one and a half seconds out of two, he could control his muscles. For half a second at a time, he could not. But he poked a pill into Allison's mouth.

"Swallow it!" he commanded. "Swallow!"

The ground-car rested tranquilly on the highway, which here went on for a mile and then dipped in a gentle incline and then rose once more. The totally level fields to right and left came to an end, here. Native trees grew, trailing preposterously long fronds. Brushwood hid much of the ground. That looked normal. But the lower, ground-covering vegetation was wilted and rotting.

Allison choked upon the pellet. Calhoun forced a second upon him. Murgatroyd looked inquisitively at first one and then the other of the two men. He said:

"*Chee? Chee?*"

Calhoun lay back in his seat, breathing carefully to keep alive. But he couldn't do anything about his heart-beat. The sun shone brightly, though now it was low, toward the horizon. There were clouds in the reddened sky. A gentle breeze blew. Everything, to outward appearance, was peaceful and tranquil and commonplace upon this small world. But in the area that human beings had taken over there were cities which were still and silent and deserted, and somewhere—somewhere!—the population of the planet waited uneasily for the latest of a series of increasingly terrifying phenomena to come to an end. Up to this time the strange, creeping, universal affliction had begun at one

101

place, and moved slowly to another, and then diminished and ceased to be. But this was the greatest and worst of the torments. And it hadn't ended. It hadn't diminished. After three days it continued at full strength at the place where previously it had stopped and died away.

The people of Maya were frightened. They couldn't return to their homes. They couldn't go anywhere. They hadn't prepared for an emergency to last for days. They hadn't brought supplies of food.

It began to look as if they were going to starve.

4.

Calhoun was in very bad shape when the sports car came to the end of the highway. First, all the multiple roadways of the route that had brought him here were joined by triple ribbons of road-surface from the north. For a space there were twenty-four lanes available to traffic. They flowed together, and then there were twelve. Here there was evidence of an enormous traffic concentration at some time now past. Brush and small trees were crushed and broken where cars had been forced to travel off the hard-surface roadways and through undergrowth. The twelve lanes dwindled to six, and the unpaved area on either side showed that innumerable cars had been forced to travel off the highway altogether. Then there were three lanes, and then two, and finally only a single ribbon of pavement where no more than two cars could run side by side. The devastation on either hand was astounding. All visible vegetation for half a mile to right and left was crushed and tangled. And then the narrow surfaced road ceased to be completely straight. It curved around a hillock—and here the ground was no longer perfectly flat—and came to an end. And Calhoun saw all the ground-cars of the planet gathered and parked together.

There were no buildings. There were no streets. There was nothing of civilization but tens and scores of thousands of ground-cars. They were extraordinary to look at, stopped at random, their fronts pointed in all directions, their air-column tubes thrusting into the ground so that there might be trouble getting them clear again.

Parked bumper to bumper and in closely-placed lines, in theory twenty-five thousand cars could be parked on a square mile of ground. But there were very many times that number of cars here, and some places were unsuitable for parking, and there were lanes placed at random and there'd been no special effort to put the maximum number of cars in the smallest place. So the surface transportation system of the planet Maya spread out over some fifty sprawling square miles. Here, cars were crowded closely. There, there was much room between them. But it seemed that as far as one could see in the twilight there were glistening vehicles gathered confusedly, so there was nothing else to be seen but an occasional large tree rising from among them.

Calhoun came to the end of the surfaced road. He'd waited for the pellets he'd taken and given to Allison to have the effect they'd had on Murgatroyd. That had come about. He'd driven on. But the strength of the inductor-field had increased to the intolerable. When he stopped the sports-car he showed the effects of what he'd been through.

Figures on foot converged upon him, instantly. There were eager calls.

"It's stopped? You got through? We can go back?"

Calhoun shook his head. It was just past sunset and many brilliant colorings showed in the western sky, but they couldn't put color into Calhoun's face. His cheeks were grayish and his eyes were deep-sunk, and he looked like someone in the last stages of exhaustion. He said heavily:

"It's still there. We came through. I'm Med Service. Have you got a government here? I need to talk to somebody who can give orders."

If he'd asked two days earlier there would have been

no answer, because the fugitives were only waiting for a disaster to come to an end. One day earlier, he might have found men with authority busily trying to arrange for drinking-water for something like two millions of people, in the entire absence of wells or pumps or ways of making either. And if he'd been a day later, it is rather likely that he'd have found savage disorder. But he arrived at sundown three days after the flight from the cities. There was no food to speak of, and water was drastically short, and the fugitives were only beginning to suspect that they would never be able to leave this place, and that they might die here.

Men left the growing crowd about the sports-car to find individuals who could give orders. Calhoun stayed in the car, resting from the unbearable strain he'd undergone. The ground-inductor cattle-fence had been ten miles deep. One mile was not bad. Only Murgatroyd had noticed it. After two miles Calhoun and Allison suffered. But the medication strengthened them to take it. But there'd been a long, long way in the center of the induction-field in which existence was pure torment. Calhoun's muscles defied him for part of every two-second cycle, and his heart and lungs seemed constantly about to give up even the pretense of working. In that part of the cattle-fence field, he'd hardly dared drive faster than a crawl, in order to keep control of the car when his own body was uncontrollable. But presently the field-strength lessened and ultimately ended.

Now Murgatroyd looked cordially at the figures who clustered about the car. He'd hardly suffered at all. He'd had half as much of the medication as Calhoun himself, and his body-weight was only a tenth of Calhoun's. He'd made out all right. Now he looked expectantly at what became a jammed mass of crowding men about the vehicle that had come through the invisible barrier across the highway. They hoped desperately for news to produce hope. But Murgatroyd waited zestfully for somebody to welcome him and offer him cakes and sweets, and undoubtedly presently a cup of coffee. But nobody did.

It was a long time before there was a stirring at the edge of the crowd. Night had fully fallen then, and for miles and miles in all directions lights in the ground-cars of Maya's inhabitants glowed brightly. They drew upon broadcast power, naturally, for their motors and their lights. Somewhere, men shouted. Calhoun turned on his headlights for a guide. More shoutings. A knot of men struggled to get through the crowd. With difficulty, presently, they reached the car.

"They say you got through," panted a tall man, "but you can't get back. They say—."

Calhoun roused himself. Allison, beside him, stirred. The tall man panted again:

"I'm the planetary president. What can we do?"

"First, listen," said Calhoun tiredly.

He'd had a little rest. Not much, but some. The actual work he'd done in driving three-hundred-odd miles from Maya City was trivial. But the continuous and lately violent spasms of his heart and breathing muscles had been exhausting. He heard Murgatroyd say ingratiatingly, "*Chee-chee-chee-chee*," and put his hand on the little animal to quiet him.

"The thing you ran away from," said Calhoun effortfully, "is a type of ground-induction field using broadcast power from the grid. It's used on Texia to confine cattle to their pastures and to move them where they're wanted to be. But it was designed for cattle. It's a cattle-fence. It could kill humans."

He went on, his voice gaining strength and steadiness as he spoke. He explained, precisely, how a ground-induction field was projected in a line at a right angle to its source. It could be moved by adjustments of the apparatus by which it was projected. It had been designed to produce the effects they'd experienced on cattle, but now it was being used on men.

"But—but if it uses broadcast power," the planetary

president said urgently, "then if the power broadcast is cut off it has to stop! If you got through it coming here, tell us how to get through going back and we'll cut off the power-broadcast ourselves! We've got to do something immediately! The whole planet's here! There's no food! There's no water! Something has to be done before we begin to die!"

"But," said Calhoun, "if you cut off the power you'll die anyway! You've got a couple of million people here. You're a hundred miles from places where there's food! Without power you couldn't get to food or bring it here. Cut the power and you're still stranded here. Without power you'll die as soon as with it."

There was a sound from the listening men around. It was partly a growl and partly a groan.

"I've just found this out," said Calhoun. "I didn't know until the last ten miles exactly what the situation was, and I had to come here to be sure. Now I need some people to help me. It won't be pleasant. I may have enough medication to get a dozen people back through. It'll be safer if I take only six. Get a doctor to pick me six men. Good heart action. Sound lungs. Two should be electronics engineers. The others should be good shots. If you get them ready, I'll give them the same stuff that got us through. It's desensitizing medication, but it will do only so much. Try and find some weapons for them."

Voices murmured all around. Men hastily explained to other men what Calhoun had said. The creeping disaster before which they'd all fled,—it was not a natural catastrophe, but an artificial one! Men had made it! They'd been herded here and their wives and children were hungry because of something men had done!

A low-pitched, buzzing, humming sound came from the crowd about the sports car. For the moment, nobody asked what could be the motive for men to do what had been done. Pure fury filled the mob. Calhoun leaned closer to Allison.

"I wouldn't get out of the car if I were you," he said

in a low tone. "I certainly wouldn't try to buy any real property at a low price!"

Allison shivered. There was a vast, vast stirring as the explanation passed from man to man. Figures moved away in the darkness. Lighted car-windows winked as they moved through the obscurity. The population of Maya was spread out over very many square miles of what had been wilderness, and there was no elaborate communication system by which information could be spread quickly. But long before dawn there'd be nobody who didn't know that they'd fled from a man-made danger and were held here like cattle, behind a cattle-fence, apparently to die.

Allison's teeth chattered. He was a business man and up to now he'd thought as one. He'd made decisions in offices, with attorneys and secretaries and clerks to make the decisions practical and safe, but without anybody to point out any consequences other than financial ones. But he saw possible consequences to himself, here and now. He'd landed on Maya because he considered the matter too important to trust to anybody else. Even riding with Calhoun on the way here, he'd only been elated and astonished at the success of the intended coup. He'd raised his aim. For a while he'd believe that he'd end as the sole proprietor of the colony on Maya, with every plant growing for his profit, and every factory earning money for him, and every inhabitant his employee. It had been the most grandiose possible dream. The details and the maneuvers needed to complete it flowed into his mind.

But now his teeth chattered. At ten words from Calhoun he would literally be torn to pieces by the raging men about him. His attache-case with millions of credits in cash,—. It would be proof of whatever Calhoun chose to say. Allison knew terror down to the bottom of his soul. But he dared not move from Calhoun's side. A single sentence in the calmest of voices would destroy him. And he'd never faced actual, understood, physical danger before.

Presently men came, one by one, to take orders from Calhoun. They were able-bodied and grim-faced men. Two were electronics engineers, as he'd specified. One was a policeman. There were two mechanics and a doctor who was also amateur tennis champion of the planet. Calhoun doled out to them the pellets that reduced the sensitiveness of muscles to externally applied stimuli. He gave instructions. They'd go as far into the cattle-fence as they could reasonably endure. Then they'd swallow the pellets and let them act. Then they'd go on. His stock of pellets was limited. He could give three to each man.

Murgatroyd squirmed disappointedly as this briefing went on. Obviously, he wasn't to make a social success here. He was annoyed. He needed more space. Calhoun tossed Allison's attache-case behind the front-seat backs. Allison was too terrified to protest. It still did not increase the space left on the front seat between Calhoun and Allison.

Four humming ground-cars lifted eight inches from the ground and hovered there on columns of rushing air. Calhoun took the lead. His headlights moved down the single-lane road to which two joining twelve-lane highways had shrunk. Behind him, other headlights moved into line. Calhoun's car moved away into the darkness. The others followed.

Brilliant stars shone overhead. A cluster of a thousand suns, two thousand light-years away, made a center of illumination that gave Maya's night the quality of a vivid if diffused moonlight. The cars went on. Presently Calhoun felt the twitchings of minor muscular spasms. He was riding into the field which had been first devised for purposes remote from the herding of cattle or humans, but applied to the first use on the planet Texia, and now applied to the second here.

The road became two, and then four, and then eight

lanes wide. Then four lanes swirled off to one side, and the remaining four presently doubled, and then widened again, and it was the twelve-lane turnpike that had brought Calhoun here from Maya City.

But the rythmic interference with his body grew stronger. Allison had spoken not one single word while Calhoun conferred with the people of Maya beyond the highway. His teeth chattered as they started back. He didn't attempt to speak during the beginning of the ride through the cattle-fence field. His teeth chattered, and stopped, and chattered again, and at long last he panted despairingly:

"Are you going to let the thing kill me?"

Calhoun stopped. The cars behind him stopped. He gave Allison two pellets and took two himself. With Murgatroyd insistently accompanying him, he went along the cars which trailed him. He made sure the six men he'd asked for took their pellets and that they had an adequate effect. He went back to the sports car.

Allison whimpered a little when he and Murgatroyd got back in.

"I thought," said Calhoun conversationally, "that you might try to take off by yourself, just now. It would solve a problem for me.—Of course it wouldn't solve any for you. But I don't think your problems have any solution, now."

He started the car up again. It moved forward. The other cars trailed dutifully. They went on through the starlit night. Calhoun noted that the effect of the cattle-fence was less than it had been before. The first desensitizing pellets had not wholly lost their effect when he added more. But he kept his speed low until he was certain the other drivers had endured the anguish of passing through the cattle-fence field.

Presently he was confident that the cattle-field was past. He sent his car up to eighty miles an hour. The other cars followed faithfully. To a hundred. They did not drop behind. The car hummed through the night at top speed,—a hundred and twenty, a hundred and thirty miles an hour. The three other cars' headlights faithfully kept pace with him.

Allison said desperately:

"Look! I—don't understand what's happened. You talk as if I'd planned all this. I—did have advance notice of a—a research project here. But it shouldn't have held the people there for days! Something went wrong! I only believed that people would want to leave Maya. I'd only planned to buy as much acreage as I could, and control of as many factories as possible. That's all! It was business! Only business!"

Calhoun did not answer. Allison might be telling the truth. Some business men would think it only intelligent to frighten people into selling their holdings below a true value. Something of the sort happened every day in stock exchanges. But the people of Maya could have died!

For that matter, they still might. They couldn't return to their homes and food so long as broadcast power kept the cattle-fence in existence. But they couldn't return to their homes and food supplies if the power-broadcast was cut off, either.

Over all the night-surface of the world of Maya there was light only on one highway at one spot, and a multitude of smaller, lesser lights where the people of Maya waited to find out whether they would live or die.

5.

Calhoun considered coldly. They were beyond what had been the farthest small city on the multiple highway. They would go on past now starlit fields of plants native to Maya, passing many places where trucks loaded with the plants climbed up to the roadway and headed for the factories which made use of them. The fields ran for scores of miles along the highway's length. They reached out beyond the horizon,—perhaps scores of miles in that direction, too. There were thousands upon thousands of square miles devoted to the growing of dark-green vegetation which supplied the raw materials for Maya's space-exports. Some hundred-odd miles ahead, the small town of Tenochitlan lay huddled in the light of a distant star-cluster. Beyond that, more highway and Maya City. Beyond that—.

Calhoun reasoned that the projector to make the induction cattle-fence would be beyond Maya City, somewhere in the mountains the space-photograph in the spaceport building showed. A large highway went into those mountains for a limited distance only. A ground-inductor projector field always formed at a right angle to the projector which was its source. It could be adjusted—the process was analogous of focussing—to come into actual being at any distance desired, and the distance could be changed. To drive the people of Maya City eastward, the projector of a cattle-fence—about which they would know nothing; it would be totally strange and completely mysterious—the projector of the cattle-fence would need to be west of the people to be driven. Logically, it would belong in the mountains. Practically, it would be concealed. Drawing on broadcast power to do its work, there would be no large power-source needed to give it the six million kilowatts it required. It should be quite easy to hide beyond any quick or easy discovery. Hunting it out might require days or weeks of searching. But the people beyond the end of the highway couldn't wait. They had no food, and holes scrabbled down to ground-water by men digging with their bare hands simply would not be adequate. The cattle-fence had to be cut off immediately. The broadcast of power had to be continued.

Calhoun made an abrupt grunting noise. Phrasing the thing that needed to be done was practically a blue-print of how to do it. Simple! He'd need the two electronics engineers, of course. But that would be the trick. . . .

He drove on at a hundred thirty miles an hour with his lips set wrily. The three other cars came behind him.

Murgatroyd watched the way ahead. Mile after mile, half-minute after half-minute, the headlights cast brilliantly blinding beams before the cars. Murgatroyd grew bored. He said, *"Chee!"* in a discontented fashion and tried to curl up between Allison and Calhoun. There wasn't room. He crawled over the seatback. He moved about, back there. There were rustling sounds. He settled down. Presently there was silence. Undoubtedly he had draped his furry tail across his nose and gone soundly off to sleep.

Allison spoke suddenly. He'd had time to think, but he had no practice in various ways of thinking.

"How much money have you got?" he asked.

"Not much," said Calhoun. "Why?"

"I—haven't done anything illegal," said Allison, with an unconvincing air of confidence, "but I could be put to some inconvenience if you were to accuse me before others of what you've accused me personally. You seem to think that I planned a highly criminal act. That the action I know of—the research project I'd heard of— that it became—that it got out of hand is likely. But I am entirely in the clear. I did nothing in which I did not have the advice of counsel. I am legally unassailable. My lawyers—."

"That's none of my business," Calhoun told him. "I'm a medical man. I landed here in the middle of what seemed to be a serious public-health situation. I went to see what had happened. I've found out. I still haven't the answer, —not the whole answer anyway. But the human population of Maya is in a state of some privation, not to say danger. I hope to end it. But I've nothing to do with anybody's guilt or innocence of crime or criminal intent or anything else."

Allison swallowed. Then he said with smooth confidence:

"But you could cause me inconvenience. I would appreciate it if you would—would—."

"Cover up what you've done?" asked Calhoun.

"No. I've done nothing wrong. But you could simply use discretion. I landed by parachute to complete some business deals I'd arranged months ago. I will go through with them. I will leave on the next ship. That's perfectly open and above-board. Strictly business. But you could make a—an unpleasing public image of me. Yet I have done nothing any other business man wouldn't do. I did happen to know of a research project—."

"I think," said Calhoun without heat, "that you sent men here with a cattle-fence device from Texia to frighten the people on Maya. They wouldn't know what was going on. They'd be scared. They'd want to get away. So you'd be able to buy up practically all the colony for the equivalent of peanuts. I can't prove that," he conceded, "but that's my opinion. But you want me not to state it. Is that right?"

"Exactly!" said Allison. He'd been shaken to the core, but he managed the tone and the air of a dignified man of business discussing an unpleasant subject with fine candor. "I assure you you are mistaken. You agree that you can't prove your suspicions. If you can't prove them, you shouldn't state them. That is simple ethics. You agree to that!"

Calhoun looked at him curiously.

"Are you waiting for me to tell you my price?"

"I'm waiting," said Allison reprovingly, "for you to agree not to cause me embarrassment. I won't be ungrateful. After all, I'm a person of some influence. I could do a great deal to your benefit. I'd be glad—."

"Are you working around to guess at a price I'll take?" asked Calhoun with the same air of curiosity.

He seemed much more curious than indignant, and much more amused than curious. Allison sweated suddenly. Calhoun didn't appear to be bribable. But Allison knew desperation.

"If you want to put it that way,—yes," he said harshly. "You can name your own figure. I mean it!"

"I won't say a word about you," said Calhoun. "I won't

need to. The characters who're operating your cattle-fence will do all the talking that's necessary. Things all fit together,—except for one item. They've been dropping into place all the while we've been driving down this road."

"I said you can name your own figure!" Allison's voice was shrill. "I mean it! Any figure! Any!"

Calhoun shrugged.

"What would a Med Ship man do with money? Forget it!"

He drove on. The highway turn-off to Tenochitlan appeared. Calhoun went steadily past it. The other connection with the road through the town appeared. He left it behind.

Allison's teeth chattered again.

The buildings of Maya City began to appear, some twenty minutes later. Calhoun slowed and the other cars closed up. He opened a window and called:

"We want to go to the landing-grid first. Somebody lead the way!"

A car went past and guided the rest assuredly to a ramp down from the now-elevated road, and through utterly dark streets, of which some were narrow and winding, and came out abruptly where the landing-grid rose skyward. At the bottom its massive girders looked huge and cyclopean in the starlight, but the higher courses looked like silver lace against the stars.

They went to the control-building. Calhoun got out. Murgatroyd hopped out after him. A bit of paper clung to his fur. He shook himself, and a five-thousand-credit interstellar credit certificate fell to the ground. Murgatroyd had made a soft place for sleeping out of the contents of Allison's attache case. It was assuredly the most expensive if not the most comfortable sleeping-cushion a *tormal* ever had. Allison sat still as if numbed. He did not even pick up the certificate.

"I need you two electronics men," said Calhoun. Then he said apologetically to the others: "I only figured out something on the way here. I'd believed we might have to take some drastic action, come daybreak. But now I doubt it. I do suggest, though, that you turn off the car headlights and get set to do some shooting if anybody turns up. I don't know whether they will or not."

He led the way inside. He turned on lights. He went to the place where dials showed the amount of power actually being used of the enormous amount available. Those dials now showed an extremely small power-drain, considering that the cities of a planet depended on the grid. But the cities were dark and empty of people. The demand-needle wavered back and forth, rhythmically. Every two seconds the demand for power went up by six million kilowatts, approximately. The demand lasted for half a second, and stopped. For a second and a half the power in use was reduced by six million kilowatts. During this period only automatic pumps and ventillators and freezing equipment drew on the broadcast-power for energy. Then the six-million-kilowatt demand came again. For half a second.

"The cattle-fence," said Calhoun, "works for half a second out of every two seconds. It's intermittent or it would simply paralyze animals that wandered into it. Or people. Being intermittent, it drives them out instead. There'll be tools and parts for equipment here, in case something needs repair. I want you to make something new."

The two electronics technicians asked questions.

"We need," said Calhoun, "an interruptor that will cut off the power-broadcast for the half-second the ground-induction field is supposed to be on. Then it should turn on the broadcast power for the second and a half the cattle-fence is supposed to be off. That will stop the cattle-fence effect, and I think a ground-car should be able to work with power that's available for three half-seconds out of four."

The electronics men blinked at him. Then they grinned. They set to work. Calhoun went exploring. He found a lunch-box in a desk. It had three very stale sandwiches in it. He offered them around. It appeared that nobody wanted to eat while their families—at the end of the highway—were still hungry.

The electronics men called on the two mechanics to help build something. They explained absorbedly to Calhoun that they were making a cut-off which would adjust to any sudden six-million-kilowatt demand, no matter what time-interval was involved. A change in the tempo of the cattle-fence cycle wouldn't bring it back on.

"That's fine!" said Calhoun. "I wouldn't have thought of that!"

He bit into a stale sandwich and went outside. Allison sat limply, despairingly, in his seat in the car.

"The cattle-fence is going off," said Calhoun without triumph. "The people of the city will probably begin to get here around sunrise."

"I—I did nothing legally wrong!" said Allison, dry-throated. "Nothing! They'd have to prove that I knew what the—consequences of the research-project would be. That couldn't be proved! It couldn't! So I've done nothing legally wrong. . . ."

Calhoun went inside, observing that the doctor who was also tennis champion, and the policeman who'd come to help him, were keeping keen eyes on the city and the foundations of the grid and all other places from which trouble might come.

There was a fine atmosphere of achievement in the power-control room. The power, itself, did not pass through these instruments. But relays here controlled buried massive conductors which supplied the world with power. And one of the relays had been modified. When the cattle-fence projector closed its circuit, the power went off. When the ground-inductor went off, the power went on. There was no longer a barrier across the highways leading to the east. It was more than probable that ground-cars could run on current supplied for one and a half seconds out of every two. They might run jerkily, but they would run.

116

Half an hour later, the amount of power drawn from the broadcast began to rise smoothly and gradually. It could mean only that cars were beginning to move.

Forty-five minutes later still, Calhoun heard stirrings outside. He went out. The two men on guard gazed off into the city. Something moved there. It was a ground-car, running slowly and without lights. Calhoun said undisturbedly:

"Whoever was running the cattle-fence found out their gadget wasn't working. Their lights flickered, too. They came to see what was the matter at the landing-grid. But they've seen the lighted windows. Got your blasters handy?"

But the unlighted car turned. It raced away. Calhoun shrugged.

"They haven't a prayer," he said. "We'll take over their apparatus as soon as it's light. It'll be too big to destroy, and there'll be fingerprints and such to identify them as the men who ran it. And they're not natives. When the police start to look for the strangers who were living where the cattle-fence projector was set up. . . . They can go into the jungles where there's nothing to eat, or they can give themselves up."

He moved toward the door of the control-building, once more. Allison said somehow desperately:

"They'll have hidden their equipment. You'll never be able to find it!"

Calhoun shook his head in the starlight.

"Anything that can fly can spot it in minutes. Even on the ground one can walk almost straight to it. You see, something happened they didn't count on. That's why they've left it turned on at full power. The earlier, teasing uses of the cattle-fence were low-power. Annoying, to start with, and uncomfortable the second time, and maybe somewhat painful the third. But the last time it was full power."

He shrugged. He didn't feel like a long oration. But it was obvious. Something had killed the plants of a

117

certain genus of which small species were weeds that destroyed Earth-type grasses. The ground-cover plants—and there were larger ones; Calhoun had seen one plant decaying in a florist's shop which had had to be grown in a cage—the ground-cover plants had motile stems and leaves and blossoms. They were cannibals. They could move their stems to reach, and their leaves to enclose, and their flowers to devour other plants. Perhaps small animals. The point, though, was that they had some limited power of motion. Earth-style sensitive plants and fly-catcher plants had primitive muscular tissues. The local ground-cover plants had them too. And the cattle-fence field made those tissues contract spasmodically. Powerfully. Violently. Repeatedly. Until they died of exhaustion. The full-power cattle-fence field had exterminated Mayan ground-cover plants all the way to the end of the east-bound highway. And inevitably—and very conveniently—also up to the exact spot where the cattle-fence field had begun to be projected. There would be an arrow-shaped narrowing of the wiped-out ground-cover plants where the cattle-field had been projected. It would narrow to a point which pointed precisely to the cattle-fence projector.

"Your friends," said Calhoun, "will probably give themselves up and ask for mercy. There's not much else they can do."

Then he said:

"They might even get it. D'you know, there's an interesting side effect of the cattle-fence. It kills the plants that have kept earth-type grasses from growing here. Wheat can be grown here now, whenever and as much as the people please. It should make this a pretty prosperous planet, not having to import all its bread."

*　*　*　*

The ground-cars of the inhabitants of Maya City did begin to arrive at sunrise. Within an hour after daybreak, very savagely intent persons found the projector of ground-induction and hence cattle-fence fields. They turned it off. It was a very bulky piece of equipment, and it had been set up underground. It should have been difficult to find. But it wasn't.

By noon there was still some anger on the faces of the people of Maya, but there'd been little or no damage, and life took up its normal course again. Murgatroyd appreciated the fact that things went back to normal. For him it was normal to be welcomed and petted when the Med Ship *Esclipus Twenty* touched ground. It was normal for him to move zestfully in admiring human society, and to drink coffee with great gusto, and to be stuffed with cakes and sweets to the full capacity of his expandable belly.

And while Murgatroyd moved in human society, enjoying himself hugely, Calhoun went about his business. Which, of course, was conferences with planetary health officials, politely receiving such information as they thought important, and tactfully telling them about the most recent developments in medical science as known to the Interstellar Medical Service.

TALLIEN THREE

1.

The Med Ship *Esclipus Twenty* rode in overdrive while her ship's company drank coffee. Calhoun sipped at a full cup of strong brew, while Murgatroyd the *tormal* drank from the tiny mug suited to his small, furry paws. The astrogation-unit showed the percentage of this overdrive-hop covered up to now, and the needle was almost around to the stop-pin.

There'd been a warning gong an hour ago, notifying that the end of overdrive journeying approached. Hence the coffee. When breakout came, the overdrive field should collapse and the Duhanne cells down near the small ship's keel absorb the energy which maintained it. Then *Esclipus Twenty* would appear in the normal universe of suns and stars with the abruptness of an explosion. She should be somewhere near the sun Tallien. She should then swim toward that sol-type sun and approach Tallien's third planet out at the less-than-light-speed rate necessary for solar-system travel. And presently she would signal down to ground and Calhoun set about the purpose of his three-week journey in overdrive. His purpose was a routine check-up on public health on Tallien Three. Calhoun had lately completed five such planetary visits, with from one to three weeks of overdrive travel between each pair. When he left Tallien Three he'd head back to Sector Headquarters for more orders about the work of the Interstellar Medical Service.

Murgatroyd zestfully licked his empty cup to get the last least drop of coffee. He said hopefully:

"Chee?" He wanted more.

"I'm afraid," said Calhoun, "that you're a sybarite, Murgatroyd. This impassioned desire of yours for coffee disturbs me."

"Chee!" said Murgatroyd, with decision.

"It's become a habit," Calhoun told him severely. "You should taper off. Remember, when anything in your environment becomes a normal part of your environment, it becomes a necessity. Coffee should be a luxury, to be savored as such, instead of something you expect and resent being deprived of."

Murgatroyd said impatiently:

"Chee-chee!"

"All right, then," said Calhoun, "if you're going to be emotional about it! Pass your cup."

He reached out and Murgatroyd put the tiny object in his hand. He refilled it and passed it back.

"But watch yourself," he advised. "We're landing on Tallien Three. It's just been transferred to us from another sector. It's been neglected. There's been no Med Service inspection for years. There could be misunderstandings."

Murgatroyd said, *"Chee!"* and squatted down to drink.

Calhoun looked at a clock and opened his mouth to speak again, when a taped voice said abruptly:

"When the gong sounds, breakout will be five seconds off."

There was a steady, monotonous tick, tock, tick, tock, like a metronome. Calhoun got up and made a casual examination of the ship's instruments. He turned on the vision-screens. They were useless in overdrive, of course. Now they were ready to inform him about the normal cosmos as soon as the ship returned to it. He put away the coffee things. Murgatroyd was reluctant to give up his mug until the last possible lick. Then he sat back and elaborately cleaned his whiskers.

Calhoun sat down in the control-chair and waited.

"Bong!" said the loud-speaker, and Murgatroyd scuttled under a chair. He held on with all four paws and his

121

furry tail. The speaker said, *"Breakout in five seconds . . . four . . . three . . . two . . . one. . . ."*

There was a sensation as if all the universe had turned itself inside out and Calhoun's stomach tried to follow its example. He gulped, and the feeling ended, and the vision-screens came alight. Then there were ten thousand myriads of stars, and a sun flaming balefully ahead, and certain very bright objects nearby. They would be planets, and one of them showed as a crescent.

Calhoun checked the solar spectrum as a matter of course. This was the sun Tallien. He checked the brighter specks in view. Three were planets and one a remote brilliant star. The crescent was Tallien Three, third out from its sun and the Med Ship's immediate destination. It was a very good breakout; too good to be anything but luck. Calhoun swung the ship for the crescent planet. He matter-of-factly checked the usual items. He was going in at a high angle to the ecliptic, so meteors and bits of stray celestial trash weren't likely to be bothersome. He made other notes, to kill time.

He re-read the data-sheets on the planet. It had been colonized three hundred years before. There'd been trouble establishing a human-use ecological system on the planet because the native plants and animals were totally useless to humankind. Native timber could be used in building, but only after drying-out for a period of months. When growing or green it was as much water-saturated as a sponge. There had never been a forest fire here; not even caused by lightning!

There were other oddities. The aboriginal micro-organisms here did not attack wastes of introduced terrestrial types. It had been necessary to introduce scavenger organisms from elsewhere. This and other difficulties made it true that only one of the world's five continents was human-occupied. Most of the land-surface was strictly as it had been before the landing of men, —impenetrable jungles of sponge-like flora, dwelt in by a largely unknown because useless fauna. Calhoun read

on. Population . . . government . . . health statistics. . . .
He went through the list.

He still had time to kill, so he re-checked his course and
speed relative to the planet. He and Murgatroyd had din-
ner. Then he waited until the ship was near enough to
report in.

"Med Ship *Esclipus Twenty* calling ground," he said
when the time came. He taped his own voice as he made
the call. "Requesting coördinates for landing. Our mass is
fifty tons. Repeat, five-oh tons. Purpose of landing, planetary health inspection."

He waited while his taped voice repeated and re-
repeated the call. An incoming voice said sharply:

"*Calling Med Ship! Cut your signal! Do not acknowledge this call! Cut your signal! Instructions will follow.
But cut your signal!*"

Calhoun blinked. Of all possible responses to a landing
call, orders to stop signalling would be least likely. But
after an instant he reached over and stopped the transmission of his voice. It happened to end half-way
through a syllable.

Silence. Not quite silence, of course, because there
was the taped record of background-noise which went
on all the time the Med Ship was in space. Without it,
the utter absence of noise would be sepulchral.

The voice from outside said:

"*You cut off. Good! Now listen! Do not—repeat, do
not!—acknowledge this call or respond to any call from
anyone else! There is a drastic situation aground. You
must not—repeat, must not—fall into the hands of the
people now occupying Government Center! Go into
orbit. We will try to seize the space-port so you can be
landed. But do not acknowledge this call or respond to
any answer from anyone else! Don't do it! Don't do it!*"

There was a click, and somehow the silence was clam-
orous. Calhoun rubbed his nose reflectively with his finger. Murgatroyd, bright-eyed, immediately rubbed his
nose with a tiny dark digit. Like all *tormals*, he gloried in

imitating human actions. But suddenly a second voice called in, with a new and strictly professional tone.

"*Calling Med Ship!*" said this second voice. "*Calling Med Ship! Space-port Tallien Three calling Med Ship Esclipus Twenty! For landing, repair to coördinates—.*"

The voice briskly gave specific instructions. It was a strictly professional voice. It repeated the instructions with precision.

Out of sheer habit, Calhoun said, "Acknowledge." Then he added sharply: "Hold it! I've just had an emergency-call—"

The first voice interrupted stridently:

"*Cut your signal, you fool! I told you not to answer any other call! Cut your signal!*"

The strictly professional other voice said coldly:

"*Emergency call, eh? That'll be paras. They're better organized than we thought, if they picked up your land-ing-request! There's an emergency, all right! It's the devil of an emergency,—it looks like devils! But this is the space-port. Will you come in?*"

"Naturally," said Calhoun. "What's the emergency?"

"*You'll find out—*" That was the professional voice. The other snapped angrily, "*Cut your signal!*" The professional voice again: "*. . . you land. It's not—.*" "*Cut your signal, you fool! Cut it—*"

There was confusion. The two voices spoke together. Each was on a tight beam, while Calhoun's call was broadcast. The voices could not hear each other, but each could hear Calhoun.

"*Don't listen to them! There's—*" "*to understand, but—*" "*Don't listen! Don't—*" " *. . when you land.*"

Then the voice from the space-port stopped, and Calhoun cut down the volume of the other. It continued to shout, though muffled. It bellowed, as if rattled. It mouthed commands as if they were arguments or reasons. Calhoun listened for fully five minutes. Then he said carefully into his microphone:

"Med Ship *Esclipus Twenty* calling space-port. I will
124

arrive at given coördinates at the time given. I suggest that you take precautions if necessary against interference with my landing. Message ends."

He swung the ship around and aimed for the destination with which he'd been supplied,—a place in emptiness five diameters out with the center of the sun's disk bearing so-and-so and the center of the planet's disk bearing so-and-thus. He turned the communicator-volume down still lower. The miniature voice shouted and threatened in the stillness of the Med Ship's control-room. After a time Calhoun said reflectively:

"I don't like this, Murgatroyd! An unidentified voice is telling us—and we're Med Ship personnel, Murgatroyd! —who we should speak to and what we should do. Our duty is plainly to ignore such orders. But with dignity, Murgatroyd! We must uphold the dignity of the Med Service!"

Murgatroyd said skeptically:

"*Chee?*"

"I don't like your attitude," said Calhoun, "but I'll bear in mind that you're often right."

Murgatroyd found a soft place to curl up in. He draped his tail across his nose and lay there, blinking at Calhoun above the furry half-mask.

The little ship drove on. The disk of the planet grew large. Presently it was below. It turned as the ship moved, and from a crescent it became a half-circle and then a gibbous near-oval shape. In the rest of the solar system nothing in particular happened. Small and heavy inner planets swam deliberately in their short orbits around the sun. Outer, gas-giant planets floated even more deliberately in larger paths. There were comets of telescopic size, and there were meteorites, and the sun Tallien sent up monstrous flares, and storms of improbable snow swept about in the methane atmosphere of the greater gas-giant of this particular celestial family of this sun and its satellites. But the cosmos in general paid no attention to human activities or usually undesirable intentions. Calhoun listened, frowning, to the agitated, commanding voice. He still didn't like it.

Suddenly, it cut off. The Med Ship approached the planet to which it had been ordered by Sector Headquarters now some months ago. Calhoun examined the nearing world via electron telescope. On the hemisphere rolling to a position under the Med Ship he saw a city of some size, and he could trace highways, and there were lesser human settlements here and there. At full magnification he could see where forests had been cut away in wedges and half-squares, with clear spaces between them. This indicated cultivated ground, cleared for human use in the invincibly tidy-minded manner of men. Presently he saw the landing-grid near the biggest city,—that half-mile-high, cage-like wall of intricately braced steel girders. It tapped the planet's ionosphere for all the power that this world's inhabitants could use, and applied the same power to lift up and let down the ships of space by which communication with the rest of humanity was maintained. From this distance, though, even with an electron telescope, Calhoun could see no movement of any sort. There was no smoke, because electricity from the grid provided all the planet's power and heat, and there were no chimneys. The city looked like a colored map, with infinite detail but nothing which stirred.

A tiny voice spoke. It was the voice of the space-port.

"Calling Med Ship. Grid locking on. Right?"

"Go ahead," said Calhoun. He turned up the communicator.

The voice from the ground said carefully:

"Better stand by your controls. If anything happens down here you may need to take emergency action."

Calhoun raised his eyebrows. But he said:

"All set."

He felt the cushiony, fumbling motions as force-fields from the landing-grid groped for the Med Ship and centered it in their complex pattern. Then there came the sudden solid feeling when the grid locked on. The Med

126

Ship began to settle, at first slowly but with increasing speed, toward the ground below.

It was all very familiar. The shapes of the continents below him were strange, but such unfamiliarity was commonplace. The voice from the ground said matter-of-factly:

"We think everything's under control, but it's hard to tell with these paras. They got away with some weather-rockets last week and may have managed to mount war-heads on them. They might use them on the grid, here, or try for you."

Calhoun said:

"What are paras?"

"You'll be briefed when you land," said the voice. It added, *"Everything's all right so far, though."*

The *Esclipus Twenty* went down and down and down. The grid had locked on at forty thousand miles. It was a long time before the little ship was down to thirty thousand and another long time before it was at twenty. Then more time to reach ten, and then five, and one thousand, and five hundred. When solid ground was only a hundred miles below and the curve of the horizon had to be looked for to be seen, the voice from the ground said:

"The last hundred miles is the tricky part, and the last five will be where it's tight. If anything does happen, it'll be there."

Calhoun watched through the electron telescope. He could see individual buildings now, when he used full magnification. He saw infinitesimal motes which would be ground-cars on the highways. At seventy miles he cut down the magnification to keep his field of vision wide. He cut the magnification again at fifty and at thirty and at ten.

Then he saw the first sign of motion. It was an extending thread of white which could only be smoke. It began well outside the city and leaped up and curved, evidently aiming at the descending Med Ship. Calhoun said curtly:

"There's a rocket coming up. Aiming at me."

The voice from the ground said:

"It's spotted. I'm giving you free motion if you want to use it."

The feel of the ship changed. It no longer descended. The landing-grid operator was holding it aloft, but Calhoun could move it in evasive action if he wished. He approved the liberty given him. He could use his emergency-rockets for evasion. A second thread of smoke came streaking upward.

Then other threads of white began just outside the landing-grid. They rushed after the first. The original rockets seemed to dodge. Others came up. There was an intricate pattern formed by the smoke-trails of rockets rising and other rockets following, and some trails swerving dodging and others closing in. Calhoun carefully reminded himself that it was not likely that there'd be atomic war-heads. The last planetary wars had been fought with fusion weapons, and only the crews of single ships survived. The planetary populations didn't. But atomic energy wasn't much used aground, these days. Power for planetary use could be had more easily from the upper, ionized limits of atmospheres.

A pursuing rocket closed in. There was a huge ball of smoke and a flash of light, but it was not brighter than the sun. It wasn't atomic flame. Calhoun relaxed. He watched as every one of the first-ascended rockets was tracked down and destroyed by another. The last, at that, was three-quarters of the way up.

The Med Ship quivered a little as the force-fields tightened again. It descended swiftly. It came to ground. Figures came to meet Calhoun as, with Murgatroyd, he went out of the airlock. Some were uniformed. All wore the grim expressions and harried looks of men under long-continued strain.

The landing-grid operator shook hands first.

"Nice going! It could be lucky that you arrived. We normals need some luck!"

He introduced a man in civilian clothes as the planetary Minister for Health. A man in uniform was head of the planetary police. Another—.

"We worked fast after your call came!" said the grid operator. "Things are lined up for you, but they're bad!"

"I've been wondering," admitted Calhoun drily, "if all incoming ships are greeted with rockets."

"That's the paras," said the police head, grimly. "They'd rather not have a Med Service man here."

A ground-car sped across the space-port. It came at a headlong pace toward the group just outside the Med Ship. There was the sudden howl of a siren by the space-port gate. A second car leaped as if to intercept the first. Its siren screamed again. Then bright sparks appeared near the first car's windows. Blasters rasped. Incredulously, Calhoun saw the blue-white of blaster-bolts darting toward him. The men about him clawed for weapons. The grid operator said sharply:

"Get in your ship! We'll take care of this! It's paras!"

But Calhoun stood still. It was instinct not to show alarm. Actually, he didn't feel it. This was too preposterous! He tried to grasp the situation and fearfulness does not help at such a time.

A bolt crackled against the Med Ship's hull just behind him. Blasters rasped from beside him. A bolt exploded almost at Calhoun's feet. There were two men in the first-moving ground-car, and now that another car moved to head them off, one fired desperately and the other tried to steer and fire at the same time. The siren-sounding car sent a stream of bolts at them. But both cars jounced and bounced. There could be no marksmanship under such conditions.

But a bolt did hit. The two-man car dipped suddenly to one side. Its fore-part touched ground. It slued around, and its rear part lifted. It flung out its two passengers and with an effect of great deliberation it rolled over end for end and came to a stop upside down. Of its passengers, one lay still. The other struggled to his feet and began to run. Toward Calhoun. He fired desperately, again and again—.

Bolts from the pursuing car struck all round him. Then one struck him. He collapsed.

Calhoun's hands clenched. Automatically, he moved toward the other still figure, to act as a medical man does when somebody is hurt. The grid operator seized his arm. As Calhoun jerked to get free, that second man stirred. His blaster lifted and rasped. The little pellet of ball-lightning grazed Calhoun's side, burning away his uniform down to the skin, just as there was a grating roar of blaster-fire. The second man died.

"Are you crazy?" demanded the grid operator angrily. "He was a para! He was here to try to kill you!"

The police head snapped:

"Get that car sprayed! See if it had equipment to spread contagion! Spray everything it went near! And hurry!"

There was silence as men came from the space-port building. They pushed a tank on wheels before them. It had a hose and a nozzle attached to it. They began to use the hose to make a thick, fog-like, heavy mist which clung to the ground and lingered there. The spray had the biting smell of phenol.

"What's going on here?" demanded Calhoun angrily. "Damnation! What's going on here?"

The Minister for Health said unhappily:

"Why—we've a public-health situation we haven't been able to meet. It appears to be an epidemic of—of—we're not sure what, but it looks like demoniac possession."

2.

"I'd like," said Calhoun, "a definition. Just what do you mean by a para?"

Murgatroyd echoed his tone in an indignant, *"Chee-chee!"*

This was twenty minutes later. Calhoun had gone back into the Med Ship and treated the blaster-burn on his side. He'd changed his clothing from the scorched uniform to civilian clothing. It would not look eccentric here. Men's ordinary garments were extremely similar all over the galaxy. Women's clothes were something else.

Now he and Murgatroyd rode in a ground-car with four armed men of the planetary police, plus the civilian who'd been introduced as the Minister for Health for the planet. The car sped briskly toward the space-port gate. Masses of thick gray fog still clung to the ground where the would-be assassins' car lay on its back and where the bodies of the two dead men remained. The mist was being spread everywhere,—everywhere the men had touched ground or where their car had run. Calhoun had some experience with epidemics and emergency measures for destroying contagion. He had more confidence in the primitive sanitary value of fire. It worked, no matter how ancient the process of burning things might be. But very many human beings, these days, never saw a naked flame unless in a science class at school, where it might be shown as a spectacularly rapid reaction of oxidation. But people used electricity for heat and light and power. Mankind had moved out of the age of fire. So here on Tallien it seemed inevitable that infective material should be sprayed with antisceptics instead of simply set ablaze.

"What," repeated Calhoun doggedly, "is a para?"

The Health Minister said unhappily:

"Paras are—beings that once were sane men. They aren't sane any longer. Perhaps they aren't men any longer. Something has happened to them.—If you'd landed a day or two later, you couldn't have landed at all. We normals had planned to blow up the landing-grid so no other ship could land and be lifted off again to spread the—contagion to other worlds.—If it is a contagion."

"Smashing the landing-grid," said Calhoun practically, "may be all right as a last resort. But surely there are other things to be tried first!"

Then he stopped. The ground-car in which he rode had reached the space-port gate. Three other ground-cars waited there. One swung into motion ahead of them. The other two took up positions behind. A caravan of four cars, each bristling with blast-weapons, swept along the wide highway which began here at the space-port and stretched straight across level ground toward the city whose towers showed on the horizon. The other cars formed a guard for Calhoun. He'd needed protection before, and he might need it again.

"Medically," he said to the Minister for Health, "I take it that a para is the human victim of some condition which makes him act insanely. That is pretty vague. You say it hasn't been controlled. That leaves everything very vague indeed.—How widely spread is it?—Geographically, I mean."

"Paras have appeared," said the Minister for Health, "at every place on Tallien Three where there are men."

"It's epidemic, then," said Calhoun professionally. "You might call it pandemic. How many cases?"

"We guess at thirty per cent of the population,—so far," said the Minister for Health, hopelessly. "But every day the total goes up." He added, "Doctor Lett has some hope for a vaccine, but it will be too late for most."

Calhoun frowned. With reasonably modern medical techniques, almost any sort of infection should be stopped long before there were as many cases as that!

"When did it start? How long has it been running?"

"The first paras were examined six months ago," said the Health Minister. "It was thought to be a disease. Our best physicians examined them. They couldn't agree on a cause, they couldn't find a germ or virus ..."

"Symptoms?" asked Calhoun crisply.

"Doctor Lett phrased them in medical terms," said the Minister for Health. "The condition begins with a period of great irritability or depression. The depression is so great that suicide is not infrequent. If that doesn't happen, there's a period of suspiciousness and secretiveness,—strongly suggestive of paranoia. Then there's a craving for—unusual food. When it becomes uncontrollable, the patient is mad!"

The ground-cars sped toward the city. A second group of vehicles appeared, waiting. As the four-car caravan swept up to them, one swung in front of the car in which Calhoun and Murgatroyd rode. The others fell into line to the rear. It began to look like a respectable fighting force.

"And after madness?" asked Calhoun.

"Then they're paras!" said the Health Minister. "They crave the incredible. They feed on the abominable. And they hate us normals as—devils out of hell would hate us!"

"And after that again?" said Calhoun. "I mean, what's the prognosis? Do they die or recover? If they recover, in how long? If they die, how soon?"

"They're paras!" said the Health Minister querulously. "I'm no physician! I'm an administrator. But I don't think any recover. Certainly none die of it! They stay—what they've become."

"My experience," said Calhoun, "has mostly been with diseases that one either recovers from or dies of. A disease whose victims organize to steal weather rockets and to use them to destroy a ship—only they failed—and who carry on with an assassination-attempt, that doesn't sound like a disease. A disease had no purpose of its own. They had a purpose,—as if they obeyed one of their number."

The Minister for Health said uneasily:

"It's been suggested—that something out of the jungle causes what's happened. On other planets there are creatures which drink blood without waking their vic-

133

tims. There are reptiles who sting men. There are even insects which sting men and inject diseases. Something like that seems to have come out of the jungle. While men sleep—something happens to them! They turn into paras. Something native to this world must be responsible. The planet did not welcome us! There's not a native plant or beast that is useful to us! We have to culture soil-bacteria so Earth-type plants can grow here! We don't begin to know all the creatures of the jungle! If something comes out and makes men paras without their knowledge—"

Calhoun said mildly:

"It would seem that such things could be discovered."

The Health Minister said bitterly:

"Not this thing! It is intelligent! It hides! It acts as if on a plan to destroy us! Why—there was a young doctor who said he'd cured a para! But we found him and the former para dead when we went to check his claim! Things from the jungle had killed them! They think! They know! They understand! They're rational, and like devils—."

A third group of ground-cars appeared ahead, waiting. Like the others, they were filled with men holding blast-rifles. They joined the procession; the rushing, never-pausing group of cars from the space-port. The highway had obviously been patrolled against a possible ambush or road-block. The augmented combat group went on.

"As a medical man," said Calhoun carefully, "I question the existence of a local, non-human rational creature. Creatures develop or adapt to fit their environment. They change or develop to fit into some niche, some special place in the ecological system which is their environment. If there is no niche, no room for a specific creature in an environment, there is no such creature there. And there cannot be a place in any environment for a creature which will change it. It would be a contradiction in terms! We rational humans change the

134

worlds we occupy. Any rational creature will! So a rational animal is as nearly impossible as any creature can be. It's true that we've happened, but—another rational race? Oh, no!"

Murgatroyd said:

"*Chee!*"

The city's towers loomed higher and taller above the horizon. Then, abruptly, the fast-moving cavalcade came to the edge of the city and plunged into it.

It was not a normal city. The buildings were not eccentric. All planets but very new ones show local architectural peculiarities, so it was not odd to see all windows topped by triple arches, or quite useless pilasters in the brick walls of apartment-buildings. These would have made the city seem only individual. But it was not normal. The streets were not clean. Two windows in three had been smashed. In places Calhoun saw doors that had been broken in and splintered, and never repaired. That implied violence unrestrained. The streets were almost empty. Occasional figures might be seen on the sidewalks before the speeding ground-cars, but the vehicles never passed them. Pedestrians turned corners or dodged into doorways before the cavalcade could overtake them.

The buildings grew taller. The street-level remained empty of humans, but now and again, many storeys up, heads peered out of windows. Then high-pitched yellings came from aloft. It was not possible to tell whether they were yells of defiance or derision or despair, but they were directed at the racing cars.

Calhoun looked quickly at the faces of the men around him. The Minister for Health looked at once heartbroken and embittered. The head of the planetary police stared grimly ahead. Screechings and howlings echoed and reëchoed between the building-walls. Objects began to fall from the windows. Bottles. Pots and pans. Chairs and stools twirled and spun, hurtling downward. Everything that was loose and could be thrown from a window came down, flung by the occupants of those high dwellings. With them came outcries which were assuredly cursings.

It occurred to Calhoun that there had been a period in history when mob-action invariably meant flames. Men burned what they hated and what they feared. They also burned religious offerings to divers bloodthirsty deities. It was fortunate, he reflected wrily, that fires were no longer a matter of common experience, or burning oil and flaming missiles would have been flung down on the ground-cars.

"Is this unpopularity yours?" he asked. "Or do I have a share in it? Am I unwelcome to some parts of the population?"

"You're unwelcome to paras," said the police head coldly. "Paras don't want you here. Whatever drives them is afraid the Med Service might make them no longer paras. And they want to stay the way they are." His lips twisted. "They aren't making this uproar, though. We gathered everybody we were sure wasn't—infected into Government Center. These people were left out. We weren't sure about them. So they consider we've left them to become paras and they don't like it!"

Calhoun frowned again. This confused everything. There was talk of infection, and talk of unseen creatures come out of the jungle, making men paras and then controlling them as if by demoniac possession. There were few human vagaries, though, that were not recorded in the Med Service files. Calhoun remembered something, and wanted to be sick. It was like an infection, and like possession by devils too. There would be creatures not much removed from fiends involved, anyhow.

"I think," he said, "that I need to talk to your counter-para researchers. You have men working on the problem?"

"We did," said the police head, grimly. "But most of them turned para. We thought they'd be more dangerous than other paras, so we shot them. But it did no good.

136

Paras still turn up, in Government Center too. Now we only send paras out the south gate. They doubtless make out,—as paras."

For a time there was silence in the rushing cars, though a bedlam of howls and curses came from aloft. Then a sudden shrieking of foreseen triumph came from overhead. A huge piece of furniture, a couch, seemed certain to crash into the car in which Calhoun rode. But it swerved sharply, ran up on the sidewalk, and the couch dashed itself to splinters where the car should have been. The car went down to the pavement once more and rushed on.

The street ended. A high barrier of masonry rose up at a cross-street. It closed the highway and connected the walls of apartment-buildings on either hand. There was a gate in it, and the leading cars drew off to one side and the car carrying Calhoun and Murgatroyd ran through, and there was a second barrier ahead, but this was closed. The other cars filed in after it, Calhoun saw that windows in these apartment-buildings had all been bricked up. They made a many-storeyed wall shutting off all that was beyond them.

Men from the barrier went from car to car of the escort, checking the men who had been the escort for Calhoun. The Minister for Health said jerkily:

"Everybody in Government Center is examined at least once each day to see if they're turning para or not. Those showing symptoms are turned out the south gate. Everybody, myself included, has to have a fresh certificate every twenty-four hours."

The inner gate swung wide. The car carrying Calhoun went through. The buildings about them ended. They were in a huge open space that must once have been a park in the center of the city. There were structures which could not possibly be other than government buildings. But the population of this world was small. They were not grandiose. There were walkways and some temporary buildings obviously thrown hastily together to house a sudden influx of people.

And here there were many people. There was bright sunshine, and children played and women watched them. There were some—not many—men in sight, but most of them were elderly. All the young ones were uniformed and hastily going here or there. And though the children played gaily, there were few smiles to be seen on adult faces.

"I take it," said Calhoun, "that this is Government Center, where you collected everybody in the city you were sure was normal. But they don't all stay normal. And you consider that it isn't exactly an infection but the result of something that's done to them by—Something."

"Many of our doctors thought so," said the Minister for Health. "But they've turned para. Maybe the—Things got at them because they were close to the truth."

His head sank forward on his chest. The police head said briefly:

"When you want to go back to your ship, say so and we'll take you. If you can't do anything for us, you'll warn other planets not to send ships here."

The ground-car braked before one of those square, unornamented buildings which are laboratories everywhere in the galaxy. The Minister for Health got out. Calhoun followed him, Murgatroyd riding on his shoulder. The ground-car went away and Calhoun followed into the building.

There was a sentry by the door, and an officer of the police. He examined the Minister's one-day certificate of health. After various vision-phone calls, he passed Calhoun and Murgatroyd. They went a short distance and another sentry stopped them. A little further, and another sentry.

"Tight security," said Calhoun.

"They know me," said the Minister heavily, "but they are checking my certificate that as of this morning I wasn't a para."

"I've seen quarantines before," said Calhoun, "but never one like this! Not against disease!"

"It isn't against disease," said the Minister, thinly. "It's against Something intelligent—from the jungles—who chooses victims by reason for its own purposes."

Calhoun said very carefully:

"I won't deny more than the jungle."

Here the Minister for Health rapped on a door and ushered Calhoun through it. They entered a huge room filled with the complex of desks, cameras, and observing and recording instruments that the study of a living organism requires. The set-up for study of dead things is quite different. Here, halfway down the room's length, there was a massive sheet of glass that divided the apartment into two. On the far side of the glass there was, obviously, an asceptic-environment room now being used as an isolation-chamber.

A man paced up and down beyond the glass. Calhoun knew he must be a para because he was cut off in idea and in fact from normal humanity. The air supplied to him could be heated almost white-hot and then chilled before being introduced into the asceptic-chamber for him to breathe, if such a thing was desired. Or the air removed could be made incandescent hot so no possible germ or its spores could get out. Wastes removed would be destroyed by passage through a carbon arc after innumerable previous sterilizing processes. In such rooms, centuries before, plants had been grown from antiseptic-soaked seeds, and chicks hatched from germ-free eggs, and even small animals delivered by aseptic Caesarean section to live in an environment in which there was no living microörganism. From rooms like this men had first learned that some types of bacteria outside the human body were essential to human health. But this man was not a volunteer for such research.

He paced up and down, his hands clenching and unclenching. When Calhoun and the Minister for Health entered the outer room, he glared at them. He cursed them, though inaudibly because of the plate of glass. He hated them hideously because they were not as he was; because they were not imprisoned behind thick glass walls through which every action and almost every thought could be watched. But there was more to his hatred than that. In the midst of fury so great that his face seemed almost purple, he suddenly yawned uncontrollably.

Calhoun blinked and stared. The man behind the glass wall yawned again and again. He was helpless to stop it. If such a thing could be, he was in a paroxysm of yawning, though his eyes glared and he beat his fists together. The muscles controlling the act of yawning worked independently of the rage that should have made yawning impossible. And he was ashamed, and he was infuriated, and he yawned more violently than seemed possible.

"A man's been known to dislocate his jaw, yawning like that," said Calhoun detachedly.

A bland voice spoke behind him.

"But if this man's jaw is dislocated, no one can help him. He is a para. We cannot join him."

Calhoun turned. He found himself regarded with unctuous condescension by a man wearing glittering thick eyeglasses—and a man's eyes have to be very bad if he can't wear contacts—and a uniform with a caduceus at his collar. He was plump. He was beaming. He was the only man Calhoun had so far seen on this planet whose expression was neither despair nor baffled hate and fury.

"You are Med Service," the beaming man observed zestfully. "Of the Interstellar Medical Service, to which all problems of public health may be referred! But here we have a real problem for you! A contagious madness! A transmissible delusion! An epidemic of insanity! A plague of the unspeakable!"

The Minister for Health said uneasily:

140

"This is Doctor Lett. He was the greatest of our physicians. Now he is nearly the last."

"Agreed," said the bland man, as zestfully as before. "But now the Interstellar Medical Service sends someone before whom I should bow! Someone whose knowledge and experience and training is so infinitely greater than mine that I become abashed! I am timid! I am hesitant to offer an opinion before a Med Service man!"

It was not unprecedented for an eminent doctor to resent the implied existence of greater skill or knowledge than his own. But this man was not only resentful. He was derisive.

"I came here," said Calhoun politely, "on what I expected to be a strictly routine visit. But I'm told there's a very grave public health situation here. I'd like to offer any help I can give."

"Grave!" Doctor Lett laughed scornfully. "It is hopeless, for poor planetary doctors like myself! But not, of course, for a Med Ship man!"

Calhoun shook his head. This man would not be easy to deal with. Tact was called for.—But the sitation was appalling.

"I have a question," said Calhoun ruefully. "I'm told that paras are madmen, and there's been mention of suspicion and secretiveness which suggests schizoparanoia and—so I have guessed—the term para for those affected in this way."

"It is not any form of paranoia," said the planetary doctor, contemptuously. "Paranoia involves suspicion of everyone. Paras despise and suspect only normals. Paranoia involves a sensation of grandeur, not to be shared. Paras are friends and companions to each other. They coöperate delightedly in attempting to make normals like themselves. A paranoiac would not want anyone to share his greatness!"

Calhoun considered, and then agreed.

"Since you've said it, I see that it must be so. But my question remains. Madness involves delusions. But paras organize themselves. They make plans and take different parts in them. They act rationally for purposes they agree on,—such as assassinating me. But how can they act rationally if they have delusions? What sort of delusions do they have?"

The Minister for Health said thinly:

"Only what horrors out of the jungles might suggest! I—I cannot listen, Doctor Lett. I cannot watch, if you intend to demonstrate!"

The man with thick glasses waved an arm. The Minister for Health went hastily out. Doctor Lett made a mirthless sound.

"He would not make a medical man!—Here is a para in this aseptic room. He is an unusually good specimen for study. He was my assistant and I knew him when he was sane. Now I know him as a para. I will show you his delusion."

He went to a small culture-oven and opened the door. He busied himself with something inside. Over his shoulder he said with unction:

"The first settlers here had much trouble establishing a human-use ecology on this world. The native plants and animals were useless. They had to be replaced with things compatible with humans. Then there was more trouble. There were no useful scavengers,—and scavengers are essential! The rat is usually dependable, but rats do not thrive on Tallien. Vultures,—no. Of course not. Carrion beetles. . . . Scarabeus beetles. . . . The flies that produce maggots to do such good work in refuse disposal. . . . None thrive on Tallien Three! And scavengers are usually specialists, too. But the colony could not continue without scavengers! So our ancestors searched on other worlds, and presently they found a creature which would multiply enormously and with a fine versatility upon the wastes of our human cities. True, it smelled like an ancient Earth-animal called skunk,—butyl mercaptan. It was not pretty,—to most eyes it is revolting. But it was a scavenger and there was no waste product it would not devour."

Doctor Lett turned from the culture-oven. He had a plastic container in his hand. A faint, disgusting odor spread from it.

"You ask what the delusions of paras may be?" He grinned derisively. He held out the container. "It is the delusion that this scavenger, this eater of unclean things; this unspeakable bit of slimy squirming flesh,— paras have the delusion that it is the most delectable of foodstuffs!"

He thrust the plastic container under Calhoun's nose. Calhoun did not draw in his breath while it remained there. Doctor Lett said in mocking admiration:

"Ah! You have the strong stomach a medical man should have! The delusion of the para is that these squirming, writhing objects are delightful! Paras develop an irresistible craving for them. It is as if men on a more nearly Earthlike world developed an uncontrollable hunger for vultures and rats and—even less tolerable things. These scavengers—paras eat them! So normal men would rather die than become paras!"

Calhoun gagged in purely instinctive revulsion. The things in the plastic container were gray and small. Had they been still, they might have been no worse to look at than raw oysters in a cocktail. But they squirmed. They writhed.

"I will show you," said Doctor Lett amiably.

He turned to the glass plate which divided the room into halves. The man beyond the thick glass now pressed eagerly against it. He looked at the container with a horrible, lustful desire. The thick-eyeglassed man clucked at him, as if at a caged animal one wishes to soothe. The man beyond the glass yawned hysterically. He seemed to whimper. He could not take his eyes from the container in the doctor's hands.

"So!" said Doctor Lett.

He pressed a button. A lock-door opened. He put the

container inside it. The door closed. It could be sterilized before the door on the other side would open, but now it was arranged to sterilize itself to prevent contagion from coming out.

The man behind the glass uttered inaudible cries. He was filled with beastly, uncontrollable impatience. He cried out at the mechanism of the contagion-lock as a beast might bellow at the opening through which food was dropped into its cage.

That lock opened, inside the glass-walled room. The plastic container appeared. The man leaped upon it. He gobbled its contents, and Calhoun was nauseated. But as the para gobbled, he glared at the two who—with Murgatroyd—watched him. He hated them with a ferocity which made veins stand put upon his temples and fury empurple his skin.

Calhoun felt that he'd gone white. He turned his eyes away and said squeamishly:

"I have never seen such a thing before."

"It is new, eh?" said Doctor Lett in a strange sort of pride. "It is new! I—even I!—have discovered something that the Med Service does not know!"

"I wouldn't say the Service doesn't know about similar things," said Calhoun slowly. "There are—sometimes—on a very small scale—dozens or perhaps hundreds of victims—there are sometimes similar irrational appetites. But on a planetary scale,—no. There has never been a—an epidemic of this size."

He still looked sick and stricken. But he asked:

"What's the result of this—appetite? What does it do to a para? What change in—say—his health takes place in a man after he becomes a para?"

"There is no change," said Doctor Lett blandly. "They are not sick and they do not die because they are paras. The condition itself is no more abnormal than—than diabetes! Diabetics require insulin. Paras require —something else. But there is prejudice against what paras need! It is as if some men would rather die

144

than use insulin and those who did use it became out-castes! I do not say what causes this condition. I do not object if the Minister for Health believes that jungle-creatures creep out and—make paras out of men." He watched Calhoun's expression. "Does your Med Service information agree with that?"

"No-o-o," said Calhoun. "I'm afraid it inclines to the idea of a monstrous cause, and it isn't much like diabetes."

"But it is!" insisted lett. "Everything digestible, no matter how unappetizing to a modern man, has been a part of the regular diet of some tribe of human savages! Even prehistoric Romans ate dormice cooked in honey! Why should the fact that a needed substance happens to be found in a scavenger—."

"The Romans didn't crave dormice," said Calhoun. "They could eat them or leave them alone."

The man behind the thick glass glared at the two in the outer room. He hated them intolerably. He cried out at them. Blood-vessels in his temples throbbed with his hatred. He cursed them—.

"I point out one thing more," said Doctor Lett. "I would like to have the coöperation of the Interstellar Medical Service. I am a citizen of this planet, and not without influence. But I would like to have my work approved by the Med Service. I submit that in some areas on ancient Earth, iodine was put into the public water-supply systems to prevent goiters and cretinism. Fluorine was put into drinking-water to prevent caries. On Tralee the public water-supply has traces of zinc and cobalt added. These are necessary trace elements. Why should you not concede that here there are trace elements or trace compounds needed—."

"You want me to report that," said Calhoun, flatly. "I couldn't do it without explaining—a number of things. Paras are madman, but they organize. A symptom of privation is violent yawning. This—condition appeared only six months ago. This planet has been colonized for three hundred years. It could not be a naturally needed trace compound."

Doctor Lett shrugged, eloquently and contemptuously.

"Then you will not report what all this planet will certify," he said curtly. "My vaccine—"

"You would not call it a vaccine if you thought it supplied a deficiency—a special need of the people of Tallien."

Doctor Lett grinned again, derisively.

"Might I not supply the deficiency and call it a vaccine? But it is not a true vaccine. It is not yet efficient. It has to be taken regularly or it does not protect."

Calhoun felt as if he had gone a little pale.

"Would you give me a small sample of your vaccine?"

"No," said Doctor Lett blandly. "The little that is available is needed for high officials who must be protected from the para condition at all costs. I am making ready to turn it out in large quantities to supply all the population. Then I will give you—suitable dosage. You will be glad to have it."

Calhoun shook his head.

"Don't you see why Med Service considers that this sort of thing has a monstrous cause? Are you the monster, Doctor Lett?" Then he said sharply, "How long have you been a para? Six months?"

Murgatroyd said, *"Chee! Chee! Chee!"* in great agitation, because Doctor Lett seized a dissecting scalpel from a table-top and crouched to spring upon Calhoun. Calhoun said:

"Easy, Murgatroyd! He won't do anything regrettable!"

He had a blaster in his hand, bearing directly on the greatest and most skilful physician of Tallien Three. And Doctor Lett did not do anything. But his eyes showed the fury of a madman.

Five minutes later, or possibly less, Calhoun went out to where the Minister for Health paced miserably up and down the corridor outside the laboratory. The Minister looked white and sick, as if despite himself he'd been picturing the demonstration Lett would have given Calhoun. He did not meet Calhoun's eyes. He said uneasily:

"I'll take you to the Planetary President, now."

"No," said Calhoun. "I got some very promising information from Dr. Lett. I want to go back to my ship first."

"But the President wants to see you!" protested the Minister for Health. "There's something he wants to discuss!"

"I want," said Calhoun, "to have something to discuss with him. There is intelligence back of this para business. I'd almost call it a demoniac intelligence. I want to get back to my ship and check on what I got from Doctor Lett."

The Minister for Health hesitated, and then said urgently:

"But the President is extremely anxious—."

"Will you," asked Calhoun politely, "arrange for me to be taken back to my ship?

The Minister for Health opened his mouth and closed it. Then he said apologetically and—it seemed to Calhoun—fearfully:

"Doctor Lett has been our only hope of conquering this—this epidemic. The President and the Cabinet felt that they had to—give him full authority. There was no other hope! We didn't know you'd come. So—Doctor Lett wished you to see the President when you left him. It won't take long!"

Calhoun said grimly:

"And he already has you scared! I begin to suspect I haven't even time to argue with you!"

"I'll get you a car and driver as soon as you've seen the President. It's only a little way!"

Calhoun growled and moved toward the exit from the laboratory. Past the sentries. Out to the open air. Here was the wide clear space which once had been a park for the city and the site of the government buildings of Tallien Three. A little distance away, children played gaily. But there were women who watched them with deep anxiety. This particular space contained all the people considered certainly free of the para syndrome. Tall buildings surrounded the area which once had been tranquil and open to all the citizens of the planet. But now those buildings were converted into walls to shut out all but the chosen,—and the chosen were no better off for having been someone's choice.

"The capitol building's only yonder," said the Minister, at once urgently and affrightedly and persuasively. "It's only a very short walk! Just yonder!"

"I still," said Calhoun, "don't want to go there." He showed the Minister for Health the blaster he'd aimed at Doctor Lett only minutes ago. "This is a blaster," he said gently. "It's adjusted for low power so that it doesn't necessarily burn or kill. It's the adjustment used by police in case of riot. With luck, it only stuns. I used it on Doctor Lett," he added unemotionally. "He's a para. Did you know? The vaccine he's been giving to certain high officials to protect them against becoming paras,—it satisfies the monstrous appetite of paras without requiring them to eat scavengers. But it also produces that appetite. In fact, it's one of the ways by which paras are made."

The Minister for Health stared at Calhoun. His face went literally gray. He tried to speak, and could not.

Calhoun added again, as unemotionally as before:

"I left Doctor Lett unconscious in his laboratory, knocked out by a low-power blaster-bolt. He knows he's a para. The President is a para, but with a supply of 'vaccine' he can deny it to himself. By the look on your face you've just found out you can't deny it to yourself any longer. You're a para, too."

The Minister for Health made an inarticulate sound. He literally wrung his hands.

"So," said Calhoun, "I want to get back to my ship and see what I can do with the 'vaccine' I took from Doctor Lett. Do you help me or don't you?"

The Minister for Health seemed to have shriveled inside his garments. He wrung his hands again. Then a ground-car braked to a stop five yards away. Two uniformed men jumped out. The first of them jerked at his blaster in its holster on his hip.

"That's the *tormal!*" he snapped. "This's the man, all right!"

Calhoun pulled the trigger of his blaster three times. It whined instead of rasping, because of its low-power setting. The Minister of Health collapsed. Before he touched ground the nearer of the two uniformed men seemed to stumble with his blaster halfway drawn. The third man toppled.

"Murgatroyd!" said Calhoun sharply.

"*Chee!*" shrilled Murgatroyd. He leaped into the ground-car beside Calhoun.

The motor squealed because of the violence with which Calhoun applied the power. It went shrilly away with three limp figures left behind upon the ground. But there wouldn't be instant investigation. The atmosphere in Government Center was not exactly normal. People looked apprehensively at them. But Calhoun was out of sight before the first of them stirred.

"It's the devil," said Calhoun as he swung to the right at a roadway-curve, "It's the devil to have scruples! If I'd killed Lett in cold blood, I'd have been the only hope these people could have. Maybe they'd have let me help them!"

He made another turn. There were buildings here and there, and he was often out of sight from where

149

he'd dropped three men. But it was astonishing that action had been taken so quickly after Lett regained consciousness. Calhoun had certainly left him not more than a quarter of an hour before. The low-power blaster must have kept him stunned for minutes. Immediately he'd recovered he'd issued orders for the capture or the killing of a man with a small animal with him, a *tormal*. And the order would have been carried out if Calhoun hadn't happened to have his own blaster actually in his hand.

But the appalling thing was the over-all situation as now revealed. The people of Government Center were turning para and Doctor Lett had all the authority of the government behind him. He was the government for the duration of the emergency. But he'd stay the government because all the men in high office were paras who could conceal their condition only so long as Doctor Lett permitted it. Calhoun could picture the social organization to be expected. There'd be the tyrant; the absolute monarch at its head. Absolutely submissive citizens would receive their dosage of vaccine to keep them "normals" so long as it pleased their master. Anyone who defied him or even tried to flee would become something both mad and repulsive, because subject to monstrous and irresistible appetites. And the tyrant could prevent even their satisfaction! So the citizens of Tallien Three were faced with an ultimate choice of slavery or madness for themselves and their families.

Calhoun swerved behind a government building and out of the parking area beyond. Obviously, he couldn't leave Government Center by the way he'd entered it. If Lett hadn't ordered him stopped, he'd be ordering it now. And Murgatroyd was an absolute identification.

Again he turned a corner, thrusting Murgatroyd down out of sight. He turned again, and again. . . . Then he began concentratedly to remember where the sunset-line had been upon the planet when he was waiting to be landed by the grid. He could guess at an hour and a half, perhaps two, since he touched ground. On the combined data, he made a guess at the local time. It would be mid-afternoon. So shadows would lie to the north-east of the objects casting them. Then—.

He did not remain on any straight roadway for more than seconds. But now when he had a choice of turnings, he had a reason for each choice. He twisted and dodged about—once he almost ran into children playing a ritual game—but the sum total of his movements was steadily southward. Paras were turned out of the south gate. That gate, alone, would be the one where someone could go out with a chance of being unchallenged.

He found the gate. The usual tall buildings bordered it to left and right. The actual exit was bare concrete walls slanting together to an exit to the outer world no more than a house-door wide. Well back from the gate, there were four high-sided trucks with armed police in the truck-bodies. They were there to make sure that paras, turned out, or who went out of their own accord when they knew their state, would not come back.

He stopped the ground-car and tucked Murgatroyd under his coat. He walked grimly toward the narrow exit. It was the most desperate of gambles, but it was the only one he could make. He could be killed, of course, but nobody would suspect him of attempting exit at any gate. He should be too desperate to take a chance like this.

So he got out, unchallenged. The concrete walls rose higher and higher as he walked away from the trucks and the police who would surely have blasted him had they guessed. The way he could walk became narrower. It became a roofed-over passageway, with a turn in it so it could not be looked through end to end. Then, —he reached open air once more.

Nothing could be less dramatic than his actual escape. He simply walked out. Nothing could be less remarkable than his arrival in the city outside of Government Center. He found himself in a city street, rather narrow, with buildings as usual all about him, whose windows were either bricked shut or smashed. There were benches against the base of one of those buildings, and four or five men, quite unarmed, lounged upon them. When Calhoun appeared one of them looked up and then arose. A second man turned to busy himself with something behind him. They were not grim. They showed no sign of being mad. But Calhoun had already realized that the appetite which was madness came only occasionally. Only at intervals which could probably be known in advance. Between one monstrous hunger-spell and another, a para might look and act and actually be as sane as anybody else. Certainly Doctor Lett and the President and the Cabinet-members who were paras acted convincingly as if they were not.

One of the men on the benches beckoned.

"This way," he said casually.

Murgatroyd poked his head out of Calhoun's jacket. He regarded these roughly dressed men with suspicion.

"What's that?" asked one of the five.

"A pet," said Calhoun briefly.

The statement went unchallenged. A man got up, lifting a small tank with a hose. There was a hissing sound. The spray made a fine, fog-like mist. Calhoun smelled a conventional organic solvent, well-known enough.

"This's antiseptic," said the man with the spray. "In case you got some disease inside there."

The statement was plainly standard, and once it had been exquisite irony. But it had been repeated until it had no meaning any more, except to Calhoun. His clothing glittered momentarily where the spray stood on its fibres. Then it dried. There was the faintest possible residue, like a coating of impalpable dust. Calhoun guessed its significance and the knowledge was intolerable. But he said between clenched teeth:

"Where do I go now?"

"Anywheres," said the first man. "Nobody'll bother you. Some normals try to keep you from getting near 'em, but you can do as you please." He added disinterestedly. "To them, too. No police out here!"

He went back to the bench and sat down. Calhoun moved on.

His inward sensations were unbearable, but he had to continue. It was not likely that instructions would have reached the para organization yet. There was one. There must be one! But eventually he would be hunted for even on the unlikely supposition that he'd gotten out of Government Center. Not yet, but presently.

He went down the street. He came to a corner and turned it. There were again a few moving figures in sight. There might be one pedestrian in a city block. This was the way they'd looked in the other part of the city, seen from a ground-car. On foot, they looked the same. Windows, too, were broken. Doors smashed in. Trash on the streets. . . .

None of the humans in view paid any attention to him at all, but he kept Muragtroyd out of sight regardless. Walking men who came toward him never quite arrived. They turned off on other streets or into doorways. Those who moved in the same direction never happened to be overtaken. They also turned corners or slipped into doors. They would be, Calhoun realized dispassionately, people who still considered themselves normals, out upon desperate errands for food and trying hopelessly not to take contagion back to those they got the food for. And Calhoun was shaken with a horrible rage that such things could happen. He, himself, had been sprayed with something. . . . And Doctor Lett had held out a plastic container for him to smell. . . . He'd held his breath then, but he could not keep from

153

breathing now. He had a certain period of time, and that period only, before—.

He forced his thoughts back to the Med Ship when it was twenty miles high, and ten, and five. He'd watched the ground through the electron telescope and he had a mental picture of the city from the sky. It was as clear to him as a map. He could orient himself. He could tell where he was.

A ground-car came to a stop some distance ahead. A man got out, his arms full of bundles which would be food. Calhoun broke into a run. The man tried to get inside the doorway before Calhoun could arrive. But he would not leave any of the food.

Calhoun showed his blaster.

"I'm a para," he said quietly, "and I want this car. Give me the keys and you can keep the food."

The man groaned. Then he dropped the keys on the ground. He fled into the house.

"Thanks," said Calhoun politely to the emptiness.

He took his place in the car. He thrust Murgatroyd again out of sight.

"It's not," he told the *tormal* with a sort of despairing humor, "It's not that I'm ashamed of you, Murgatroyd, but I'm afraid I may become ashamed of myself. Keep low!"

He started the car and drove away.

He passed through a business district, with many smashed windows. He passed through cañons formed by office buildings. He crossed a manufacturing area, in which there were many ungainly factories but no sign of any work going on. In any epidemic many men stay home from work to avoid contagion. On Tallien Three nobody would be willing to risk employment, for fear of losing much more than his life.

Then there was a wide straight highway leading away from the city but not toward the space-port. Calhoun drove his stolen car along it. He saw the strange steel embroidery of the landing-grid rising to the height of a minor mountain against the sky. He drove furiously. Beyond it. He had seen the highway system from twenty miles height, and ten, and five. From somewhere near here stolen weather-rockets had gone bellowing skyward with explosive war-heads to shatter *Esclipus Twenty*.

They'd failed. Now Calhoun went past the place from which they had been launched, and did not notice. Once he could look across flat fields and see the space-port highway. It was empty. Then there was sunset. He saw the topmost silvery beams and girders of the landing-grid still glowing in sunshine which no longer reached down to the planet's solid ground.

He drove. And drove. In Government Center nobody would suspect him long gone from the Center and driving swiftly away from the city. They might put a road-block to the space-port, just in case. But they'd really believe him still hiding somewhere in Government Center with no hope of—actually—accomplishing anything but his own destruction.

After sunset he was miles beyond the space-port. When twilight was done, he'd crossed to another surface-road and was headed back toward the city. But this time he would pass close to the space-port. And two hours after sundown he turned the car's running-lights off and drove a dark and nearly noiseless vehicle through deep-fallen night. Even so, he left the ground-car a mile from the tall and looming lace-work of steel. He listened with straining ears for a long time.

Presently he and Murgatroyd approached the space-port, on foot, from a rather improbable direction. The gigantic, unsubstantial tower rose incredibly far toward the sky. As he drew near it he crouched lower and lower so he was almost crawling to keep from being silhouetted against the stars. He saw lights in the windows of the grid's control-building. As he looked, a lighted window darkened from someone moving past it inside. There was an enormous stillness, broken only

155

by faint, faint noises of the wind in the metal skeleton.

He saw no ground-cars to indicate men brought here and waiting for him. He went very cautiously forward. Once he stopped and distastefully restored his blaster to lethal-charge intensity. If he had to use it, he couldn't hope to shoot accurately enough to stun an antagonist. He'd have to fight for his life,—or rather, for the chance to live as a normal man, and to restore that possibility to the people in the ghastly-quiet city at the horizon and the other lesser cities elsewhere on this world.

He took infinite precautions. He saw the Med Ship standing valiantly upright on its landing-fins. It was a relief to see it. The grid operator could have been ordered to lift it out to space,—thrown away to nowhere, or put in orbit until it was wanted again, or—.

That was still a possibility. Calhoun's expression turned wry. He'd have to do something about the grid. He must be able to take off on the ship's emergency rockets without the risk of being caught by the tremendously powerful force-fields by which ships were launched and landed.

He crept close to the control-building. No voices, but there was movement inside. Presently he peered in a window.

The grid operator who'd been the first man to greet him on his landing, now moved about the interior of the building. He pushed a tank on wheels. With a hose attached to it, he sprayed. Mist poured out and splashed away from the side-walls. It hung in the air and settled on the desks, the chairs, and on the control-board with its dials and switches. Calhoun had seen the mist before. It had been used to spray instead of burning the bodies of the two men who'd tried to murder him, and their wrecked ground-car, and everywhere that the car was known to have run. It was a decontaminant spray; credited with the ability to destroy the contagion that made paras out of men.

156

Calhoun saw the grid operator's face. It was resolute beyond expression, but it was very, very bitter.

Calhoun went confidently to the door and knocked on it. A savage voice inside said:

"Go away! I just found out I'm a para!"

Calhoun opened the door and walked inside. Murgatroyd followed. He sneezed as the mist reached his nostrils.

"I've been treated," said Calhoun, "so I'll be a para right along with you, after whatever the development period is. Question; can you fix the controls so nobody else can use the grid?"

The grid operator stared at him numbly. He was deathly pale. He did not seem able to grasp what Calhoun had said.

"I've got to do some work on the para condition," Calhoun told him. "I need to be undisturbed in the ship, and I need a patient further along toward being a para than I am. It'll save time. If you'll help, we may be able to beat the thing. If not, I've still got to disable the grid."

The grid operator said in a savage, unhuman voice:

"I'm a para. I'm trying to spray everything I've touched. Then I'm going to go off somewhere and kill myself—."

Calhoun drew his blaster. He adjusted it again to non-lethal intensity.

"Good man!" he said approvingly. "I'll have a similar job to do if I'm not a better medical man than Lett! Will you help me?"

Murgatroyd sneezed again. He said plaintively:

"*Chee!*"

The grid operator looked down at him, obviously in a state of shock. No ordinary sight or sound could have gotten through to his consciousness. But Murgatroyd was a small, furry animal with long whiskers and a hirsute tail and a habit of imitating the actions of humans. He sneezed yet again and looked up. There was a handkerchief in Calhoun's pocket. Murgatroyd dragged it

157

out and held it to his face. He sneezed once more and said, *"Chee!"* and returned the handkerchief to its place. He regarded the grid operator disapprovingly. The operator was shocked out of his despair. He said shakenly:

"What the devil—." Then he stared at Calhoun. "Help you? How can I help anybody? I'm a para!"

"Which," said Calhoun, "is just what I need. I'm Med Service, man! I've got a job to do with what they call an epidemic. I need a para who's willing to be cured. That's you! Let's get this grid fixed so it can't work and—."

There was a succession of loud clicks from a speaker-unit on the wall. It was an emergency-wave, unlocking the speaker from its off position. Then a voice:

"All citizens attention! The Planetary President is about to give you good news about the end of the para epidemic!"

A pause. Then a grave and trembling voice came out of the speaker:

"My fellow-citizens, I have the happiness to report that a vaccine completely protecting normals against the para condition, and curing those already paras, has been developed. Doctor Lett, of the planetary health service, has produced the vaccine which is already in small-scale production and will shortly be available in large quantities, enough for everyone! The epidemic which has threatened every person on Tallien Three is about to end! And to hasten the time when every person on the planet will have the vaccine in the required dosage and at the required intervals, Doctor Lett has been given complete emergency authority. He is empowered to call upon every citizen for any labor, any sum, any sacrifice that will restore our afflicted fellow-citizens to normality, and to protect the rest against falling a victim to this intolerable disease. I repeat: a vaccine has been found which absolutely prevents anyone from becoming a para, and which

cures those who are paras now. And Doctor Lett has absolute authority to issue any orders he feels necessary to hasten the end of the epidemic and to prevent its return. But the end is sure!"

The speaker clicked off. Calhoun said wrily:

"Unfortunately, I know what that means. The President has announced the government's abdication in favor of Doctor Lett, and that the punishment for disobeying Lett is—madness."

He drew a deep breath and shrugged his shoulders. "Come along! Let's get to work!"

4.

As it happened, the timing was critical, though Calhoun hadn't realized it. There were moving lights on the highway to the city at the moment Calhoun and the grid operator went into the Med Ship and closed the airlock door behind them. The lights drew nearer. They raced. Then ground-cars came rushing through the gate of the space-port and flung themselves toward the wholly peaceful little Med Ship where it stood seeming to yearn toward the sky. In seconds they had it ringed about, and armed men were trying to get inside. But Med Ships land on very many planets, with very many degrees of respect for the Interstellar Medical Service. On some worlds there is great integrity displayed by space-port personnel and visitors. On others there is pilfering, or worse. So Med Ships are not easily broken into.

They spent long minutes fumbling unskilfully at the outer airlock door. Then they gave it up. Two car-loads of men went over to the control-building, which now was dark and silent. Its door was not locked. They went in.

There was consternation. The interior of the control-building reeked of antiseptic spray,—the spray used when a para was discovered. In some cases, the spray a para used when he discovered himself. But it was not reassuring to the men just arrived from Government Center. Instead of certifying to their safety, it told of horrifying danger. Because despite a broadcast by the planetary president, terror of paras was too well-established to be cured by an official statement.

The men who'd entered the building stumbled out and stammered of what they'd smelled inside the building. Their companions drew back, frightened by even so indirect a contact with supposed contagion. They stayed outside, while a man who hadn't entered used the police-car's communicator to report to the headquarters of the planetary police.

The attempt to enter the ship was known inside, of course. But Calhoun paid no attention. He emptied the pockets of the garments he'd worn into the city. There were the usual trivia a man carries with him. But there was also a blaster—set for low-power bolts—and a small thick-glass phial of a singular grayish fluid, and a plastic container.

He was changing to other clothing when he heard the muttering report, picked up by a ship-receiver tuned to planetary police wave-length. It reported affrightedly that the Med Ship could not be entered, and the grid's control-building was dark and empty and sprayed as if to destroy contagion. The operator was gone.

Another voice snapped orders in reply. The highest authority had given instructions that the Med Ship man now somewhere in the capitol city must be captured, and his escape from the planet must be prevented at all costs. So if the ship itself could not be entered and disabled, get the grid working and throw it away. Throw it out to space! Whether there was contagion in the control-building or not, the ship must be made unusable to the Med Ship man!

"They think well of me," said Calhoun. "I hope I'm as dangerous as Doctor Lett now believes." Then he said crisply, "You say you're a para. I want the symptoms; how you feel and where. Then I want to know your last contact with scavengers."

The intentions of the police outside could be ignored. It wouldn't matter if the Med Ship were heaved out to space and abandoned. Calhoun was in it. But it couldn't happen. The grid operator had brought away certain essential small parts of the grid control-system. Of course the ship could be blown up. But he'd have warning of that. He was safe except for one thing. He'd been exposed to whatever it was that made a man a para. The condition would develop. But he did have a thick-glass container of grayish fluid, and he had a plastic biological-specimen container. One came from Doctor Lett's safest pocket. It would be vaccine. The other came from the culture-oven in the Doctor's laboratory.

The thick-glass phial was simply that. Calhoun removed the cover from the other. It contained small and horrible squirming organisms, writhing in what was probably a nutrient fluid to which they could reduce human refuse. They swam jerkily in it so that the liquid seemed to seethe. It smelled. Like skunk.

The grid operator clenched his hands.

"Put it away!" he commanded fiercely. "Out of sight! Away!"

Calhoun nodded. He locked it in a small chest. As he put down the cover he said in an indescribable tone:

"It doesn't smell as bad to me as it did."

But his hands were steady as he drew a sample of a few drops from the vaccine-bottle. He lowered a wall-panel and behind it there was a minute but astonishingly complete biological laboratory. It was designed for micro-analysis,—the quantitative and qualitative analysis of tiny quantities of matter. He swung out a miniaturized Challis fractionator. He inserted half a droplet of the supposed vaccine and plugged in the fractionator's power cable. It began to hum.

The grid operator ground his teeth.

"This is a fractionator," said Calhoun. "It spins a biological sample through a chromatograph gele."

The small device hummed more shrilly. The sound rose in pitch until it was a whine, and then a whistle, and then went up above the highest pitch to which human ears are sensitive. Murgatroyd scratched at his ears and complained:

"Chee! Chee! Chee!"

"It won't be long," Calhoun assured him. He looked once at the grid operator and then looked away. There was sweat on the man's forhead. Calhoun said casually, "The substance that makes the vaccine do what it does do is in the vaccine, obviously. So the fractionator is separating the different substances that are mixed together." He added, "It doesn't look much like chromatography, but the principle's the same. It's an old, old trick!"

It was, of course. That different dissolved substances can be separated by their different rates of diffusion through wetted powders and geles had been known since the early twentieth century, but was largely forgotten because not often needed. But the Med Service did not abandon processes solely because they were not new.

Calhoun took another droplet of the vaccine and put it between two plates of glass, to spread out. He separated them and put them in a vacuum-drier.

"I'm not going to try an analysis," he observed. "It would be silly to try to do anything so complicated if I only need to identify something. Which I hope is all I do need!"

He brought out an extremely small vacuum device. He cleaned the garments he'd just removed, drawing every particle of dust from them. The dust appeared in a transparent tube which was part of the machine.

"I was sprayed with something I suspect the worst

162

of," he added. "The spray left dust behind. I *think* it made sure that anybody who left Government Center would surely be a para. It's another reason for haste."

The grid operator ground his teeth again. He did not really hear Calhoun. He was deep in a private hell of shame and horror.

The inside of the ship was quiet, but it was not tranquil. Calhoun worked calmly enough, but there were times when his inwards seemed to knot and cramp him, which was not the result of any infection or contagion or demoniac possession, but was reaction to thoughts of the imprisoned para in the laboratory. That man had gobbled the unspeakable because he could not help himself, but he was mad with rage and shame over what he had become. Calhoun could become like that—.

The loud-speaker tuned to outside frequencies muttered again. Calhoun turned up its volume.

"Calling headquarters!" panted a voice. *"There's a mob of paras forming in the streets in the Mooreton quarter! They're raging! They heard the President's speech and they swear they'll kill him! They won't stand for a cure! Everybody's got to turn para! They won't have normals on the planet! Everybody's got to turn para or be killed!"*

The grid operator looked up at the speaker. The ultimate of bitterness appeared on his face. He saw Calhoun's eyes on him and said savagely:

"That's where I belong!"

Murgatroyd went to his cubbyhole and crawled into it.

Calhoun got out a microscope. He examined the dried glass plates from the vacuum-drier. The fractionator turned itself off and he focussed on and studied the slide it yielded. He inspected a sample of the dust he'd gotten from the garments that had been sprayed at the south gate. The dust contained common dust-particles and pollen-particles and thread-particles and all sorts of microscopic debris. But throughout all the sample he saw certain infinitely tiny crystals. They were too small to be seen separately by the naked eye, but they had a definite crystalline form. And the kind of crystals a substance makes are not too specific about what the substance is, but they tell a great deal about what it cannot be. In the fractionator-slide he could get more information,—the rate-of-diffusion of a substance in solution ruled out all but a certain number of compounds that it could be. The two items together gave a definite clue.

Another voice from the speaker:

"*Headquarters! Paras are massing by the north gate! They act ugly! They're trying to force their way into Government Center! We'll have to start shooting if we're to stop them! What are our orders?*"

The grid operator said dully:

"They'll wreck everything. I don't want to live because I'm a para, but I haven't acted like one yet. Not yet! But they have! So they don't want to be cured! They'd never forget what they've done . . . They'd be ashamed!"

Calhoun punched keys on a very small computer. He'd gotten an index-of-refraction reading on crystals too small to be seen except through a microscope. That information, plus specific gravity, plus crystalline form, plus rate of diffusion in a fractionator, went to the stores of information packed in the computer's memory-banks somewhere between the ship's living-quarters and its outer skin.

A voice boomed from another speaker, tuned to public-broadcast frequency:

"*My fellow-citizens, I appeal to you to be calm! I beg you to be patient! Practice the self-control that citizens owe to themselves and their world! I appeal to you—.*"

Outside in the starlight the Med Ship rested peacefully on the ground. Around and above it the grid rose like geometric fantasy to veil most of the starry sky. Here in the starlight the ground-car communicators gave out the same voice. The same message. The President of Tallien Three made a speech. Earlier, he'd made another. Earlier still he'd taken orders from the man who was already absolute master of the population of this planet.

Police stood uneasy guard about the Med Ship because they could not enter it. Some of their number who had entered the control-building now stood shivering outside it, unable to force themselves inside again. There was a vast, detached stillness about the spaceport. It seemed the more unearthly because of the thin music of wind in the landing-grid's upper levels.

At the horizon there was a faint glow. Street-lights still burned in the planet's capitol city, but though buildings rose against the sky no lights burned in them. It was not wise for anybody to burn lights that could be seen outside their dwellings. There were police, to be sure. But they were all in Government Center, marshalled there to try to hold a perimeter formed by bricked-up apartment buildings. But much the most of the city was dark and terribly empty save for mobs of all sizes but all raging. Nine-tenths of the city was at the mercy of the paras. Families darkened their homes and terrifiedly hid in corners and in closets, listening for outcries or the thunderous tramping of madmen at their doors.

In the Med Ship the loudspeaker went on.

"—*I have told you,*" said the rounded tones of the planetary president—but his voice shook—"*I have told you that Doctor Lett has perfected and is making a vaccine which will protect every citizen and cure every para. You must believe me, my fellow-citizens. You must believe me! To paras, I promise that their fellows who were not afflicted with the same condition,—I promise that they will forget! I promise that no one will remember what—what has been done in delirium! What*

165

*has taken place—and there have been tragedies—will be
blotted out. Only be patient now! Only—"*

Calhoun went over his glass slides again while the
computer stood motionless, apparently without life. But
he had called for it to find, in its memory-banks, an
organic compound of such-and-such a crystalline form,
such-and-such a diffusion rate, such-and-such a specific
gravity, and such-and-such a refractive index. Men no
longer considered that there was any effective limit to
the number of organic compounds that were possible.
The old guess at half a million different substances
was long exceeded. It took time even for a computer
to search all its microfilmed memories for a compound
such as Calhoun had described.

"It's standard practice," said Calhoun restlessly, "to
consider that everything that can happen, does. Specifically, that any compound that can possibly exist,
sooner or later must be formed in nature. We're looking
for a particular one. It must have been formed naturally
at some time or another, but never before has it appeared in quantity enough to threaten a civilization.
Why?"

Murgatroyd licked his right-hand whiskers. He whimpered a little,—and Murgatroyd was a very cheerful
small animal, possessed of exuberant good health and a
fine zest in simply being alive. Now, though, he did not
seem happy at all.

"It's been known for a long time," said Calhoun impatiently, "that no life-form exists alone. Every living
creature exists in an environment in association with
all the other living creatures around it. But this is true
of compounds, too! Anything that is part of an environment is essential to that environment. So even organic
compounds are as much parts of a planetary life-system
as—say—rabbits on a Terran-type world. If there are
no predators, rabbits will multiply until they starve."

Murgatroyd said, *"Chee!"* as if complaining to himself.

"Rats," said Calhoun, somehow angrily, "rats have

been known to do that on a derelict ship. There was a man named Malthus who said we humans would some day do the same thing. But we haven't. We've taken over a galaxy. If we ever crowd this, there are more galaxies for us to colonize, forever! But there have been cases of rats and rabbits multiplying past endurance. Here we've got an organic molecule that has multiplied out of all reason! It's normal for it to exist, but in a normal environment it's held in check by other molecules which in some sense feed on it; which control the —population of that kind of molecule as rabbits or rats are controlled in a larger environment. But the check on this molecule isn't working, here!"

The booming voice of the planetary president went on and on and on. Memoranda of events taking place were handed to him, and he read them and argued with the paras who had tried to rush the north gate of Government Center, to make its inhabitants paras like themselves. But the planetary president tried to make oratory a weapon against madness.

Calhoun grimaced at the voice. He said fretfully:

"There's a molecule which has to exist because it can. It's a part of a normal environment, but it doesn't normally produce paras. Now it does! Why? What is the compound or the condition that controls its abundance? Why is it missing here? What is lacking? What?"

The police-frequency speaker suddenly rattled, as if someone shouted into a microphone.

"All police cars! Paras have broken through a building-wall on the west side! They're pouring into the Center! All cars rush! Set blasters at full power and use them! Drive them back or kill them!"

The grid operator turned angry, bitter eyes upon Calhoun.

"The paras—we paras!—don't want to be cured!" he said fiercely. "Who'd want to be normal again and remember when he ate scavengers? I haven't yet, but—. Who'd be able to talk to a man he knew had devoured

—devoured—." The grid operator swallowed. "We paras want everybody to be like us, so we can endure being what we are! We can't take it any other way,—except by dying!"

He stood up. He reached for the blaster Calhoun had put aside when he changed from the clothes he'd worn in the city.

"—And I'll take it that way!"

Calhoun whirled. His fist snapped out. The grid operator reeled back. The blaster dropped from his hand. Murgatroyd cried out shrilly, from his cubbyhole. He hated violence, did Murgatroyd.

Calhoun stood over the operator, raging:

"It's not that bad yet! You haven't yawned once! You can stand the need for monstrousness for a long while yet! And I need you!"

He turned away. The President's voice boomed—. It cut off abruptly. Another voice took its place. And this was the bland and unctious voice of Doctor Lett.

"*My friends! I am Doctor Lett! I have been entrusted with all the powers of the government because I, and I alone, have all power over the cause of the para condition. From this moment I am the government! To paras, —you need not be cured unless you choose. There will be places and free supplies for you to enjoy the deep satisfactions known only to you! To non-paras,— you will be protected from becoming paras except by your own choice. In return, you will obey! The price of protection is obedience. The penalty for disobedience will be loss of protection. But those from whom protection is withdrawn will not be supplied with their necessities! Paras, you will remember this! Non-paras, do not forget it!. . . .*" His voice changed. "*Now I give an order! To the police and to non-paras. You will no longer resist paras! To paras; you will enter Government Center quietly and peacefully. You will not molest the non-paras you come upon. I begin at once the organization of a new social system in which paras and non-*

168

paras must coöperate. There must be obedience to the utmost—."

The grid operator cursed as he rose from the floor. Calhoun did not notice. The computer had finally delivered a strip of paper on which was the answer he had demanded. And it was of no use. Calhoun said tonelessly:

"Turn that off, will you?"

While the grid operator obeyed, Calhoun read and re-read the strip of tape. He had lacked something of good color before, but as he re-read, he grew paler and paler. Murgatroyd got down restlessly from his cubbyhole. He sniffed. He went toward the small locked chest in which Calhoun had put away the plastic container of living scavengers. He put his nose to the crack of that chest's cover.

"*Chee!*" he said confidently. He looked at Calhoun. Calhoun did not notice.

"This," said Calhoun, completely white. "This is bad! It's—it's an answer, but it would take time to work it out, and we haven't got the time! And to make it and to distribute it—."

The grid operator growled. Doctor Lett's broadcast had verified everything Calhoun said. Doctor Lett was now the government of Tallien Three. There was nobody who could dare to oppose him. He could make anybody into a para, and then deny that para his unspeakable necessities. He could turn anybody on the planet into a madman with ferocious and intolerable appetites, and then deny their satisfaction. The people of Tallien Three were the slaves of Doctor Lett. The grid operator said in a deadly voice:

"Maybe I can get to him and kill him before—."

Calhoun shook his head. Then he saw Murgatroyd sniffing at the chest now holding the container of live scavengers. Open, it had a faint but utterly disgusting odor. Locked up, Calhoun could not smell it. But

169

Murgatroyd could. He sniffed. He said impatiently to Calhoun:

"*Chee! Chee-chee!*"

Calhoun stared. His lips tightened. He'd thought of Murgatroyd as immune to everything, because he could react more swiftly and produce antibodies to toxins more rapidly than microörganisms could multiply. But he was immune only to toxins. He was not immune to an appetite-causing molecule which demanded more of itself on penalty of madness. In fact,—it affected him faster than it would a man.

"*Chee-chee!*" he chattered urgently. "*Chee-chee-chee!*"

"It's got him," said Calhoun. He felt sickened. "It'll have me. Because I can't synthesize anything as complex as the computer says is needed, to control—" His tone was despairing irony,—"to control the molecular population that makes paras!"

Murgatroyd chattered again. He was indignant. He wanted something and Calhoun didn't give it to him. He could not understand so preposterous a happening. He reached up and tugged at Calhoun's trouser-leg. Calhoun picked him up and tossed him the width of the control-room. He'd done it often before, in play, but this was somehow different. Murgatroyd stared incredulously at Calhoun. "To break it down," said Calhoun bitterly, "I need aromatic olefines and some acetone, and acetic-acid radicals and methyl sub-molecular groups. To destroy it absolutely I need available unsaturated hydrocarbons,—they'll be gases! And it has to be kept from re-forming as it's broken up, and I may need twenty different organic radicals available at the same time! It's a month's work for a dozen competent men just to find out how to make it, and I'd have to make it in quantity for millions of people and persuade them of its necessity against all the authority of the government and the hatred of the paras, and then distribute it—."

170

Murgatroyd was upset. He wanted something that Calhoun wouldn't give him. Calhoun had shown impatience,—almost an unheard-of thing! Murgatroyd squirmed unhappily. He still wanted the thing in the chest. But if he did something ingratiating. . . .

He saw the blaster, lying on the floor. Calhoun often petted him when, imitating, he picked up something that had been dropped. Murgatroyd went over to the blaster. He looked back at Calhoun. Calhoun paced irritably up and down. The grid operator stood with clenched hands, contemplating the intolerable and the monstrous.

Murgatroyd picked up the blaster. He trotted over to Calhoun. He plucked at the man's trouser-leg again. He held the blaster in the only way his tiny paws could manage it. A dark, sharp-nailed finger rested on the trigger.

"Chee-chee!" said Murgatroyd.

He offered the blaster. Calhoun jumped when he saw it in Murgatroyd's paw. The blaster jerked, and Murgatroyd's paw tightened to hold it. He pulled the trigger. A blaster-bolt crashed out of the barrel. It was a miniature bolt of ball-lightning. It went into the floor, vaporizing the surface and carbonizing the multi-ply wood layer beneath it. The Med Ship suddenly reeked of wood-smoke and surfacer. Murgatroyd fled in panic to his cubbyhole and cowered in its farthest corner.

But there was a singular silence in the Med Ship. Calhoun's expression was startled; amazed. He was speechless for long seconds. Then he said blankly:

"Damnation! How much of a fool can a man make of himself when he works at it? Do you smell that?" He shot the question at the grid operator. "Do you smell that? It's wood-smoke! Did you know it?"

Murgatroyd listened fearfully, blinking.

"Wood-smoke!" said Calhoun between his teeth. "And I didn't see it! Men have had fires for two million years and electricity for half a thousand. For two million

171

years there was no man or woman or child who went a full day without breathing in some wood-smoke! And I didn't realize that it was so normal a part of human environment that it was a necessary one!"

There was a crash. Calhoun had smashed a chair. It was an oddity because it was made of wood. Calhoun had owned it because it was odd. Now he smashed it to splinters and piled them up and flung blaster-bolt after blaster-bolt into the heap. The air inside the Med Ship grew pungent; stinging; strangling. Murgatroyd sneezed. Calhoun coughed. The grid operator seemed about to choke. But in the white fog Calhoun cried exultantly:

"Aromatic olefines! Acetone! Acetic-acid radicals and methyl sub-molecular groups! And smoke has unsaturated hydrocarbon gases. . . . This is the stuff our ancestors have breathed in tiny quantities for a hundred thousand generations! Of course it was essential to them! And to us! It was a part of their environment, so they had to have a use for it! And it controlled the population of certain molecules. . . ."

The air-system gradually cleared away the smoke, but the Med Ship still reeked of wood-smoke smells.

"Let's check on this thing!" snapped Calhoun. "Murgatroyd!"

Murgatroyd came timidly to the door of his cubby-hole. He blinked imploringly at Calhoun. At a repeated command he came unhappily to his master. Calhoun petted him. Then he opened the chest in which a container held living scavengers which writhed and swam and seemed to seethe. He took out that container. He took off the lid.

Murgatroyd backed away. His expression was ludicrous. There was no question but that his nose was grievously offended. Calhoun turned to the grid operator. He extended the sample of scavengers. The grid man clenched his teeth and took it. Then his face worked. He thrust it back into Calhoun's hand.

"It's—horrible!" he said thickly. "Horrible!" Then his jaw dropped. "I'm not a para! Not—a para—" Then he said fiercely. "We've got to get this thing started! We've got to start curing paras—."

"Who," said Calhoun, "will be ashamed of what they remember. We can't get coöperation from them! And we can't get coöperation from the government! The men who were the government are paras and they've given their authority to Doctor Lett. You don't think he'll abdicate, do you? Especially when it's realized that he was the man who developed the strain of scavengers that secrete this modified butyl mercaptan that turns men into paras!"

Calhoun grinned almost hysterically.

"Maybe it was an accident. Maybe he found himself the first para and was completely astonished. But he couldn't be alone in what he knew was—degradation. He wanted others with him in that ghastly state. He got them. Then he didn't want anybody not to be like himself. . . . We can't get help from him!"

Exultantly, he flipped switches to show on vision-screens what went on in the world outside the ship. He turned on all the receivers that could pick up sounds and broadcasts. Voices came in:

"*There's fighting everywhere! Normals won't accept paras among them! Paras won't leave normals alone . . . They touch them; breathe on them—and laugh! There's fighting—.*" The notion that the para state was contagious was still cherished by paras. It was to be preferred to the notion that they were possessed by devils. But there were some who gloried in the more dramatic opinion. There were screamings on the air, suddenly, and a man's voice panting, "*Send police here fast! The paras have gone wild. They're—*"

Calhoun seated himself at the control-desk. He threw switches there. He momentarily touched a button. There was a slight shock and the beginning of a roar outside. It cut off. Calhoun looked at the vision-plates showing outside. There was swirling smoke and steam. There were men running in headlong flight, leaving their ground-cars behind them.

"A slight touch of emergency-rocket," said Calhoun. "They've run away. Now we end the plague on Tallien Three."

The grid operator was still dazed by the continued absence of any indication that he might ever become a para. He said unsteadily:

"Sure! Sure! But how?"

"Wood-smoke," said Calhoun. "Emergency-rockets. Roofs! There's been no wood-smoke in the air on this planet because there are no forest fires and people don't burn fuel. They use electricity. So we start the largest production of wood-smoke that we find convenient, and the population of a certain modified butyl mercaptan molecule will be reduced. Down to a normal level. Immediately!"

The emergency-rocket bellowed thunderously, and the little Med Ship rose.

There have been, of course, emergency measures against contagion all through human history. There was a king of France, on Earth, who had all the lepers in his kingdom killed. There have been ships and houses burned to drive out plague, and quarantines which simply interfered with human beings were countless. Calhoun's measure on Tallien was somewhat more drastic than most, but it had good justification.

He set fire to the planet's capital city. The little Med Ship swept over the darkened buildings. Her emergency-rockets made thin pencils of flame two hundred feet long. She touched off roofs to the east, and Calhoun rose to see which way the wind blew. He descended and touched here and there. . . .

Thick, seemingly suffocating masses of wood-smoke flowed over the city. They were not actually strangling, but they created panic. There was fighting in Government Center, but it stopped when the mysterious stuff—

not one man in a hundred had ever seen burning wood or smelled its smoke,—the fighting stopped and all men fled when a choking, reeking blanket rolled over the city and lay there.

It wasn't a great fire, considering everything. Less than ten per cent of the city burned, but ninety-odd per cent of the paras in it ceased to be paras. More, they had suddenly regained an invincible aversion to the smell of butyl mercaptan—even a modified butyl mercaptan—and it was promptly discovered that no normal who had smelled wood-smoke became a para. So all the towns and even individual farm-houses would hereafter make sure that there was pungent wood-smoke to be smelled from time to time by everybody.

But Calhoun did not wait for such pleasant news. He could not look for gratitude. He'd burned part of a city. He'd forced paras to stop being paras and become ashamed. And those who hadn't become paras wanted desperately to forget the whole matter as soon as possible. They couldn't, but gratitude to Calhoun would remind them. He took appropriate action.

With the grid operator landed again, and after the grid was operable once more and had sent the Med Ship a good five planetary diameters into space;—some few hours after the ship was in overdrive again, Calhoun and Murgatroyd had coffee together. Murgatroyd zestfully licked his emptied tiny mug, to get the last least taste of the beverage. He said happily, *"Chee!"* He wanted more.

"Coffee," said Calhoun severely, "has become a habit with you, Murgatroyd! If this abnormal appetite develops too far, you might start yawning at me, which would imply that your desire for it was uncontrollable. A yawn caused by what is called a yen has been known to make a man dislocate his jaw. You might do that. You wouldn't like it!"

Murgatroyd said, *"Chee!"*

"You don't believe it, eh?" said Calhoun. Then he

175

said, "Murgatroyd, I'm going to spend odd moments all the rest of my life wondering about what happens to Doctor Lett! They'll kill him, somehow. But I suspect they'll be quite gentle with him. There's no way to imagine a punishment that would really fit! Isn't that more interesting than coffee?"

"*Chee! Chee! Chee!*" said Murgatroyd insistently.

"It wasn't wise to stay and try to make an ordinary public-health inspection. We'll send somebody else when things are back to normal."

"*Chee!!!*" said Murgatroyd loudly.

"Oh, all right!" said Calhoun. "If you're going to be emotional about it, pass your cup!"

He reached out his hand, Murgatroyd put his tiny mug in it. Calhoun refilled it. Murgatroyd sipped zestfully.

The Med Ship *Esclipus Twenty* went on in overdrive, back toward sector headquarters of the Interstellar Medical Service.